Please renew or return items by the date
shown on your receipt

www.hertsdirect.org/libraries

Renewals and   0300 123 4049
enquiries:

Textphone for hearing   0300 123 4041
or speech impaired

IFEONA FULANI

TEN DAYS IN JAMAICA

PEEPAL TREE

First published in Great Britain in 2012
Peepal Tree Press Ltd
17 King's Avenue
Leeds LS6 1QS
England

ISBN13: 9781845231996

Supported using public funding by
ARTS COUNCIL
ENGLAND

CONTENTS

To Charles and Madge

PRECIOUS AND HER HAIR

All Precious wanted was a boy to go to the beach with on Saturdays. She'd be strolling on the sand with a sweet-looking boy, arm in arm, the envy of all the boyless girls out there. There'd be water fights, splashing in the sea foam, she in her bikini, laughing, sea-water sparkling on her face. Then they'd watch the sun set at Ras Peter's restaurant, eating fish and festival, like tourists.

See Precious at seventeen: slender as a cane stalk, skin like caramel, full star-apple mouth. At night she tossed in bed, the sheets hot against her skin, fingers tracing the shape of her lips, travelling across her breasts and down to her thighs and the custard-apple flesh between them. Each morning she peered into the speckled wardrobe mirror, saw long legs, a narrow waist, a slender shapely body. Yet all this was nullified by a head of short, peppercorn hair that refused to grow.

The boy she really wanted was Neville Campbell, neighbour, sixthformer and school Romeo. Precious lived for glimpses of Neville. Dressed for school, she would wait behind the hibiscus bush at the entrance to her mother's yard until Neville came swaggering by. Blushing, and trembling like a periwinkle in the wind, she would fall in step beside him, he so crisp and lithe in his khaki uniform. Sometimes he smiled and said, *Morning*, but usually he just nodded and kept on walking, gazing at the road ahead. Afternoons, after school, Precious loitered on the dusty road, praying he would pass and notice her. Sometimes he did walk by, but surrounded by a cohort of raucous, jostling boys.

Precious lived with her mother, Lucille, in a house by the main road, just before it curved downhill towards the coast. Precious resembled her mother, who was slender and handsome with a neat head of low-cropped hair which she covered with a turban of pristine white cloth. Precious had many of Lucille's features, but not her mother's practicality and common sense. The two of them lived alone, her father having migrated to America ten years back. (They should have joined him long ago: he had filed for their papers, but such matters take a long time, or so he wrote in the letters sent with his monthly remittances.) Lucille fussed over Precious, her only child, her eyeball, but she was stern, not wanting to spoil her. She had ambitions for her daughter of a practical kind: sixth form, then college followed by a respectable, well-paying job. Each night, after reading her Bible, Lucille prayed softly, on her knees by the bed: *Maasa God, please bless my daughter, let her have ambition and sense. And beg you, Lord, let her turn out good.*

But at seventeen, Precious's one ambition was to be Neville's girl. Lucille took in the dreaminess, the moping over schoolwork, the mooning by the garden gate. Boy trouble! Lucille pursed her lips. It had to be that, though as far as she knew Precious had not had the opportunity to get into baby trouble – yet.

One evening, after dinner, Lucille sat her daughter down for a cautionary word.

What wrong with you these days, Precious?

Nothing, Mama.

Is that boy Neville you making cow-eye after?

N-no, Mama, said Precious, biting back a giggle.

Can't you see he's not paying you one bit of mind? A sweetboy like him, only have time for fool-fool, flighty-flighty girls. Not a decent child like you.

Y-yes, Mama. I know.

Hanging out at the beach with her best friend Lindy the following Saturday, Precious had a chance to see the truth of Lucille's words. Further along the beach Christine Chang and Selina Brown were parading on the sand in the scantiest thong bikinis, swarmed over by boys, Neville among them.

Lindy stared at Selina Brown's swivel hips, breathed from deep in her chest like her granny did when she was vexed, and sucked air through her teeth.

You see those girls? She pointed at Selina. They're good for nothing decent. They're just fly-bait for the sweet-boys.

But Precious was wondering how they did it. Christine had no bottom to speak of, and Selina's legs, thinner than green bamboo twigs, bowed gently at the knee. But they both had plentiful hair; hair that lifted in the wind and fanned around their shoulders; hair that caressed their cheeks, tempting boys to touch it.

Precious resolved to get herself more hair.

She went first to Pauline, the village postmistress, who was also the village hairdresser. Pauline's salon was no more than shack at behind her house, but it was crammed full of women waiting to get their hair done on the day Precious stopped by.

You have to help me, Pauline, said Precious. I want long hair and I need it fast!

Pauline paused in the middle of a colouring job to run her hand over Precious's head.

Hmmm, she said, shaking her crop of bouncy bronze

curls. Not much here to work with... it'll have to be braids or African twists, or a weave...?

Precious decided on braids, the least expensive option. She saved lunch money for three weeks to pay for them, feeding on visions of herself transformed into a beauty with a head of luxuriant, waving hair. On the appointed Saturday, she sweated for hours in a plastic chair in Pauline's shack. The small room was hot, the atmosphere thick with fumes from straighteners and dyes, and the smell of body odours. Sweat trickled down Precious's face and from her underarms, but she sat patient and still while Pauline wove every strand of hair into an artificially extended plait. While Pauline pulled and tugged her hair, Precious took refuge in a day-dream of herself and Neville strolling arm in arm along the sand under the jealous nose of skinny, bandy-legged Selina Brown.

When Precious stepped out of Pauline's den into the twilight, she was lightheaded with exhilaration, despite a prickling sensation on her scalp. She rushed home to dance before the mirror, laughing and swinging her new braids. She ran to wake-up her mother, who was dozing on the verandah.

Hmm... said Lucille, who did not approve of extensions. Extensions were a vanity and therefore sinful, no matter how pretty. More trouble coming, she sighed. She pursed her lips together and frowned, then fell asleep again.

That night Precious dreamed of Neville. He was swimming with long, supple strokes, swimming through waves of hair. The next morning she awoke with a smile on her lips. She stretched, tossing back her braids, and then noticed a thin black thing on her pillow, coiled like a delicately patterned snake. She shrieked and ran to the mirror, frantically feeling along her hairline. Oh my God! Oh my God! She wailed as more braids came away, leaving a bald patch the size of a ten cents piece above her right temple. The bald patch on her head or the braids in her hand, she was not sure which was worse.

Oh Mama, look what happened! She ran into Lucille's room, weeping like a child whose favourite doll had broken. Lucille sat by her dresser, her Bible open on her lap. She took in the situation with one glance.

You see where vanity lead you? Lucille sat Precious down and started undoing the remaining braids before they too fell out. But the hair the braids were attached to came away in Lucille's hands like dandelion fluff, exposing the smooth, reddened expanse of her daughter's scalp. Precious watched in the mirror, tears welling, chest heaving, wishing she were dead.

That day Precious stayed home from school. She tossed on her bed, clutching her head in passionate regret, imagining the snickering and whispering awaiting her next day. She spent a sleepless night trying hard not to visualise Neville reacting to her baldness, though a small inner voice tried to tell her that he probably wouldn't notice. The next morning, Lucille pulled her out of bed and stood over her while she dressed. Then, with a length of white fabric, Lucille wrapped a neat turban around Precious's head.

I can't go to school like this! Precious wailed.

Is either this or your bald head exposed to the entire school! Lucille said, and pushed her out the of the door.

Laughter rippled through the classroom as Precious entered, the focus of all eyes. *Precious born again!* Voices whispered, giggled and smirked. *Precious got the spirit, like her mother!* Precious paused in the doorway. A spirit did rise up in her at that moment; a spirit straightened her spine, lifted her head and lit a fire in her eyes. She scanned the room and the whispering ceased. Then, smiling as though in a trance, she glided through the silence and sat at her desk, ready for class to begin.

★

Sister Homelia lived in a solitary, tumbledown house in a hollow at the bottom of the hill. She was hardly ever seen in the village because she was too old and feeble to make the steep uphill climb. Yet everyone in the village knew of her skill with plants and herbs, and at some time in their life, most villagers found their way through the bush to Sister Homelia's house.

After school was let out, Precious headed downhill through the woods, climbing over fallen branches, dodging hungry mosquitos and flies the size of bees. There was no fence around Sister Homelia's garden, no gate or garden path, only a trail of hardened earth leading up to a listing front door.

The door opened before Precious had even raised her hand to knock.

Come in, girl, come in. Sister Homelia stood in the doorway leaning heavily on a walking stick, beckoning with her free hand. She appeared younger than Precious had imagined, her dark skin smooth and glossy, her figure slim as a girl's. But her neck crooked slightly, and her head drooped, wobbling from side to side, like a ripe jackfruit about to fall. Her faded eyes peered at Precious, neither friendly nor hostile.

Precious stepped out of the sun into a sparsely furnished room musty with the smell of drying leaves and fresh earth and recently boiled bananas.

S-sorry to trouble you Sister Homelia, Precious began, but the woman interrupted.

12

Tell me, girl, what you want? She pointed to two chairs by a table under a small, curtained window.

It's my hair… Precious sat down, and Sister Homelia hobbled to her side, extending a crusty hand to touch her head.

Is that chemical foolishness you put on your head? As if to point up the folly of such things, Sister Homelia raised a hand to her own braided grey hair.

N-no… it was extensions.

Aahmmmph! The old lady made a rattling noise deep in her throat. And now you want something to help it grow again?

Y-yes Sister. And I want it to grow long… long down my back like Christine Chang…

God give you the hair you have for a reason, don't you know that girl?

But no boy wants a girl with picky hair… like mine was.

Aahmmp! Well. If you want that kind of hair you'll have to do exactly as I tell you.

I'll do anything! Anything!

Ahmmmph!

Sister Homelia hobbled into an adjacent room, returning in a few moments with a brown paper bag.

Put a spoonful of this in a dish, mix it with some oil. Then… She bent towards Precious and whispered in her ear.

You not serious, Sister? Sweat beaded Precious's forehead.

The old woman nodded.

Start when the moon is dark and put it on every night until the moon is bright.

Every night?

Yes, every night. Then when the hair begins to grow,

you mustn't let water come near it. Not bath water, not rain water, not sea water. You hear me?

But it going to stink terrible! Precious wailed.

Aahmmph! Do you want hair, or don't you? Sister Homelia hobbled over to the door, the tap tap of her stick sending echoes through the room. She opened the door wide, and stood in the doorway, her head gently bobbing from side to side.

Can nothing else help me?

Nothing I know of.

Sister Homelia pushed the door shut.

As she scrambled through the thicket, Precious's mind was a tangle of thoughts. Could the mash of dried stuff in the brown paper bag really help her hair grow? Would it be worth the awful smell, the inconvenience? A nightly application of stinky mess and then a shampoo every morning for two whole weeks! And without her mother finding out? Who had time for all that and household chores and schoolwork besides?

But as Precious drew back her hand to throw the paper bag in the bushes, a vision of Neville arose before her: Neville smiling, so tall and alluring her breath caught in her chest, her pulse picked up speed. *Choh, you too lazy, girl, and too coward!* a voice admonished in her head. *Nothing worth having comes easy!* She sighed, and sighed again, acknowledging the wisdom of the voice. Then she stuffed the paper bag in her backpack and resumed the trek home.

★

On the night of the new moon, Precious crept out to the bathhouse after Lucille had gone to sleep, the bag of herbs in one hand, a kerosene lamp in the other. By the flickering lamplight she scanned the ground for the additional, unmentionable ingredient and was relieved to find a fresh pile, lying not far from the bathhouse door. Squatting on the bathhouse step, she mixed the slop in a worn enamel mug normally used to scoop up rainwater from the tank. She used a paintbrush to apply the slop, which trickled down her neck in thick brown streams, soiling her nightdress, so that when the operation was over she had to bathe again and wash out the nightdress. Back in her room, unable to lie down lest her messy head leave stains on the pillow for Lucille to find, she sat crosslegged on the bed and leaned her back against the wall, sleeping fitfully until dawn. She woke at cockcrow with a crick in her neck, but leaped up and ran to the bathhouse to shampoo her head before Lucille awoke. The night after, she used a plastic bag as a headwrap, to contain the latrine smell of the potion and keep the mess off her pillow. During the day, she wore a turban with such nonchalance that younger girls at school began to emulate her, establishing a trend known forever after as Precious's style.

After two weeks of nightly applications, Precious's hair began to grow. It so grew fast, by a week later a thick fuzz had sprouted all over her head. Two weeks later, a fluffy cap of tight, glossy curls covered her scalp, and four weeks later the hair touched her ears. The hair continued to grow, and each night she stood before the speckled mirror and unwrapped the turban, face rapt, blood fizzing, heart dancing in her chest. She had more hair than she'd ever had before. She scrutinized it in the mirror, turning this way and that as though uncertain it was really there. The nightly unwrapping turned into a game of surprise, for as it grew the hair seemed to change. Fuzzy at first, then curly, it eventually grew as straight and heavy as Christine Chang's. But even as she rejoiced at its length, Precious wished the hair were curly: its straightness made her face look flat, her eyes too small, and her scalp flaked and itched so badly that she was driven to raking her fingernails hard over the scaling skin.

When the hair hung past her shoulder blades, Precious decided the time had come to show it off. She planned its first appearance for the day of Ras Peter's annual fish fry, which drew crowds from nearby villages and tourist resorts along the coast. Neville and his posse would be there, along with all the local youths, who would loiter by the sound system, ogling tourist girls, and quaffing cans of chilled beer.

The night before the fish fry Precious braided the hair so it would wave by morning. She took a warm-water bath, she pumiced her feet and rubbed her skin all over with cornmeal. She painted her nails with an orange glaze sneaked from Lucille's dressing table. Before falling into bed, she ironed her favourite shorts and orange linen top and hung it on the wardrobe in readiness, like a soldier preparing for battle.

She lay awake that night, hearing harmonies in the chirrups of night creatures and the deep rustlings of leaves. She rose before daybreak and padded softly to the kitchen. She made peppermint tea, taking care not to rattle the kettle or make a noise that would wake Lucille. She felt special that morning, tender and full of promise, like a hibiscus bud about to unfurl its petals and reveal its velvet heart. She took her tea out to the back of the house and sat on the doorstep. The tree-covered hillside and the plain below were still covered with soft swirls of mist.

Let the day be fine, Precious whispered as rosy glimmerings of sunrise crept over the horizon. Then she laughed, because it was August, when rain never fell.

Please let Neville be there, she prayed, though she

knew that only serious illness or injury would keep him away.

What if something goes wrong? But it was hard to imagine what could go wrong, other than rain, or Neville not showing, but fear of the unimaginable swooped like gas in the bottom of her belly. What if something did go awry? What if all her effort failed, all the longing failed, all the potions and the headwraps of the past three months proved to be effort wasted?

Set your mind on the best! As she spoke Lucille's favourite affirmation she felt a power in the words that she'd never felt before. She straightened her spine, and shook out the hair that was both her charm and her weapon.

★

When Precious emerged from her room dressed for the fish-fry, Lucille thought she was seeing a vision in orange, swathed in waving black hair.

Oh my Lord! Where did that hair come from? She shrieked, then clapped her hand over her mouth, ashamed of her outburst.

It's all mine, Mama, come feel it. Precious proudly offered her head for her mother's touch.

Precious, is it a wig?

It's mine, Mama. Sister Homelia helped me grow it. And Precious waltzed out of the house leaving her mother collapsed on a lounger, wailing and clutching her head.

Precious waited for Lindy, leaning against the front gate, hair blowing in the light breeze, like a model.

Lindy froze in her tracks and then shrieked with laughter.

Precious, you mad or something? You mean you waste your mother's good money on a weave?

Lindy stepped to left and to right, surveying Precious's hair, arms akimbo.

Precious stared at Lindy in amazement. She had expected admiration, even envy, but not disbelief and no, not laughter!

It's all mine. Come, feel it. She offered her head to Lindy's sceptical tugs.

So how you get it to grow so long, so fast?

I got some herbal tonic from Sister Homelia. It worked good, eh? Don't you like it? She felt suddenly uncertain, her confidence wavering.

Jesus, said Lindy, wide eyed. Now I know you really mad!

The walk to the beach was not the triumphal approach Precious had anticipated, though by the time she and Lindy neared the fish fry, her spirits had began to rally. She's just jealous! Precious told herself, touching her hair. She tossed her head, swinging her hair, and pressed on towards the excitement up ahead, leaving Lindy to follow.

There were cars choking up the beach road, their stereos and radios blaring. Louder still, the bass throb of Ras Peter's sound system made a visceral wall of sound. As she moved across the sand, Precious inhaled the salty wind that carried the aroma of frying fish and the scent of rum and lime. She scanned the faces on the beach with a pounding heart. Local people were outnumbered by folks from neighbouring villages and there were tourists strewn baking on the hot sand. Let's get some fish, Lindy was saying, but Precious was not hungry. She was too close to her quarry to rest for food. And she was perspiring under all that hair. She needed to find Neville while the hair was still wavy and before she dissolved in sweat.

She saw a huddle of young people by the mountain of speakers along the beach. Shading her eyes from the sun, she made out the tall silhouette of Neville and set off towards him, her pulse beating in her ears louder than the sound system's bass throb. As she drew close to the group, two people broke away, holding hands. As they came into view, Precious froze. They were gazing into each others' faces and smiling. The girl was clearly foreign, pale and blond-haired, in a tourist's uniform of bikini briefs and a tight tank top.

Despite the heat, Precious began to tremble. She clutched her throat to stop the wail that rose from her belly and wanted to take flight on the sea breeze. Neville with a white girl! Tears spiked with anger welled in her eyes and the bitter taste of failure settled on her tongue. Not even Sister Homelia could help her now. What was she to do with Neville and the girl advancing towards her? Should she keep walking, meet them face to face, and ignore the smirk in Neville's eye? Or should she take her shame back to Lindy, who no doubt was waiting to laugh her to scorn? Her face was burning in the acid yellow heat of the sun, and her scalp itched with such intensity that she craved the cooling touch of salt water on her head. She looked longingly at the sea.

Neville and the girl were almost in front of her and she could hear their laughter rising on the wind, blending with the sea gulls' mocking cries. Precious turned on her heel, almost running towards the water. Without stopping to take off her outfit, she plunged into the sea, cleaving through its gentle waves like a large orange fish. She swam until she felt light headed, then paused to catch her breath. Treading water, she looked back towards the beach, hoping that Neville and the girl would be diminished by distance. Instead, her eye fell on a floating black mass glistening like oil spilled on the aquamarine surface of the sea. Legs pedalling frantically, Precious reached for her head. Her scalp felt clean, satin smooth to the touch. She bobbed in the water, clutching her head and gasping deep breaths until her mind became calm and her body felt light, as though relieved of a weighty burden.

The merciless sun burned down hot as a naked flame. To cool off, Precious dove underwater, surfaced, and dove again, repeatedly, like a fish escaped from a net, enjoying its freedom.

FEVERGRASS TEA

When she first moved into the house, she used to lounge on the verandah at sundown, sipping pineapple soda while the sun slid behind the mountains in a haze of purple flames. But in a matter of days her evening idyll was disrupted by one destitute woman, the first of a steady trickle of needy locals who, sighting her on the verandah, pushed at the rusty iron gate, braving the overgrowth of thorny bougainvillea, to bang on her door and beg.

Tell me, Yvonne, who's to blame? Margie her cousin and neighbour demanded when Yvonne complained. Who in their right mind would put their hand in their pocket and give that old drunken wretch Isilda *ten whole dollars* for no reason at all? Privately, Margie had thought Yvonne's charity typical of the show-off behaviour of returnees who came home from America with dollars flowing from their pockets. Three months after her arrival and many supplicants later, Yvonne was less generous. These days, as soon as she heard the creak of the gate she would call out: Sorry! Nothing to give away today!

The day Donovan pushed at her gate and entered her yard she did not call out. Something about his height, the muscular arms, the way his thick hair sprang back from his forehead, stilled her tongue.

Mornin, ma'am. He paused by the step and greeted her with a courteous nod. I'm Donovan. I live down the road, just past Chin shop. I pass here often, you know, and I can't help noticin that this yard need some attention. His voice was soft, his speech deliberate, and he looked her in the eye.

I do yard work. I can clear up this mess for you.

Oh. Yvonne raised a hand to smooth her braided hair. Well, yes, it really is a mess. She wished she were wearing something more stylish than baggy cotton pants.

I've been thinking of hiring someone to cut the grass.

I figure three days' work go fix it. His glance took in the drooping mango trees and the unkempt hedge of crotons with branches that waved in the breeze.

For a moment she pondered the wisdom of hiring a total stranger. She took in the bright white T-shirt and well-fitting jeans.

You don't look like a gardener. Her eyes narrowed.

Don't worry yourself, miss, he said with a lopsided smile. I been chopping yards from I was a little youth. This is nothing. I live in this district for years. Everybody know me. Ask Margie next door. She'll tell you.

So you know Margie? Ah. OK, then. What's your fee?

He named a sum she thought pitifully small. He was asking less for three days' labour than she charged to cut and sew a simple blouse, but that was how it was in that part of the island. Men and women chopped cane or tended fields, from dawn to sundown, for a few dollars a day. It was backwards, yes, but nothing she alone could do about it. She accepted his price. They agreed he would start work the next day, and with the briefest of nods he turned on his heel and strode away.

22

Yvonne went back indoors, intending to start work on a wedding dress for the daughter of a local politician, but her mind was racing too fast to concentrate, buzzing almost. This couldn't have anything to do with the yard man. Maybe she had made her morning coffee too strong. She sank into an easy chair beside the wide window overlooking the miniature forest that passed for a front garden. When Donovan finished clearing it she would be able to see beyond the head-high hedge of crotons, across the valley to the panoramic stretch of the Blue Mountain ridge. She eased back in the chair, one hand travelling under her T-shirt to finger the crescent-shaped scar in the crease beneath her left breast. The scar was raised and still tender to touch, though the breast that covered it was numb. The scar would heal completely, in time, the specialist had said, and she would quickly grow accustomed to the saline-filled sac that had replaced her diseased breast.

Yvonne thought of Leyla, her mother, who had taken time off from her job to nurse her through the weeks of chemotherapy. Now that she was well again, Yvonne felt ashamed at how completely illness had robbed her of adulthood, of how abjectly she had depended on her mother's care, a scared, needy child again. Leaving New York was as much about getting away from Leyla's coddling as about recuperating in the sun. Margie had come up with that idea . She had made all the arrangements; found the house, helped Yvonne to settle in, even found customers in the village, so Yvonne could earn a little money as a dressmaker. The small house was cheap to rent, and close to Margie's much larger home. It suited Yvonne, even the riot of plant life overtaking its grounds. Nature's vitality was everywhere. She heard it in the day-long noises of restless crickets, in the nighttime warbling of contented blackbirds. She saw it in the fluttering blue swarms of morning glories, measured it in the exuberant growth of every flower, shrub and tree. It was like food taken in through the senses. Yet at night she was lonely. She still ached for Martin, her ex-lover. He had promised he would visit, but she doubted he could face her after their long-distance break-up. She missed her girlfriends, going out for a pizza and a movie, the morning banter of colleagues at the studio over coffee and a bagel. There was Margie, of course, and she was lively company, but she was married, with three children and a teaching job. She had little time for entertaining her cousin.

Donovan came the next morning, before sunrise, while Yvonne was still asleep. She woke to the rhythmic *chop, chop* of his machete, and dressing quickly in shorts and a ribbed cotton top, she went outside to watch for a while. He was cutting back grass that had grown shoulder high, wielding the machete with fluid motions of arm and torso. In the pale grey light of early morning, he was a graceful, almost ethereal figure, absorbed in the work, unaware of her gaze.

She breakfasted on grapefruit, papaya and Earl Grey tea. She offered him a cup, calling out from the front window. The steady rise and fall of his cutting arm paused. He looked up, mopped the sweat from his face with a piece of old towel.

No Miss, no thanks, he said, and returned to work. She drew back from the window, piqued by his refusal, and wondered at his curtness: had she violated some local code of conduct with an offer of tea?

She took her mug into the tiny room at the back of the house where she had constructed a makeshift work table from an old door covered with a plastic sheet, and stacked-up wooden crates. A portable sewing machine took up one end of the table; the other was swathed in white satin, marked up and ready for cutting. She picked up the scissors, but the view from the window distracted her: a gently sloping hillside clad in coconut palms, their branches shimmered by the wind, their leaves refracting light. After New York's concrete grey congestion, the aquamarine sky and rich greens had a sweetly narcotic effect. How could she possibly miss the bustle of Seventh Avenue and the studio where she had pored over a drawing board for ten, twelve hours a day, six, sometimes seven days a week? She didn't miss those interminable hours. Had those long working days lowered her resistance to disease? Had stress made her ill? Had she been weakened by a diet of coffee, fast food and exhaust fumes?

She'd been happy enough in her tiny apartment on 8th Street. She stayed there twelve years, the last with Martin. Martin. His face interrupted her reverie, a quiet ache taking shape in her head. His forehead seemed always creased with worry: worry about problems at work, about money, and later on, about her health. In the end she had asked him to move out. She couldn't bear him to see her so altered, so weakened by surgery and medication. Till you get well, he had said, and she agreed. He had driven her to the airport, had held her and kissed her face. He'd promised to fly down for a few days soon, real soon. He called the morning after she landed, and every evening for a week after, then less and less frequently. It hurt that she could see his face so clearly, yet he felt remote and somehow irretrievable, part of a past unblemished by disease. Tears pricked her eyes. She blinked and shook her head, forced her attention back to the fabric on the table, took a firm grasp of the scissors and resumed cutting.

At 4 o'clock, as she was pinning sections of the dress together, she was summoned to the verandah door by a tap on the grille.

I finish for today, Miss. Donovan had changed into his regular clothes, jeans and a T-shirt. He gestured towards the now neat lawn. I'll be back Thursday, same time. He nodded and walked away.

On Thursday Donovan worked late into the evening, pushing himself to complete the job until darkness stopped him. Yvonne had downed tools at sunset. She was stretched out on a lounger, a novel open on her lap. As he approached the verandah to take his leave she noticed with a twinge of conscience that he walked with a tired droop.

Donovan, she said, rising to meet him, why not rest a minute and have a cool drink? Or some tea?

Abruptly, without a word, he turned and retraced his steps down the path, the mashed-down backs of his work-shoes flip-flapping against his heels. He stopped near the gate beside what looked like a huge clump of long, coarse grass and cut a fistful of blades with his machete.

What's this? she said when he handed them to her.

You don't know fevergrass? His eyebrows rose. Don't you know how to make fevergrass tea?

I don't. It doesn't grow in New York. Yvonne laughed.

Leaving his shoes by the doorway, Donovan followed her through the living room to the sparsely equipped kitchen at the back of the house. She sensed him taking in the freshly painted walls and polished floor tiles, and noticed he trod gingerly, almost on tiptoe, as though he were trespassing.

In the kitchen, she reached for the shiny new kettle which sat on the stove, but he stopped her.

You make this tea in a pot, he said.

Feeling ignorant, she took an enamel pan from the cupboard and handed it to him. He half-filled it with water and set it on the stove to boil.

I probably had fevergrass tea as a child, before my parents took me to the States, she said. I'll probably remember when I taste it.

He rinsed the leaves, twisted them into a thick coil and immersed it in boiling water. A rich, delicious aroma rose, filling the kitchen with a perfume of lemon and roses.

It smells good, she sighed, inhaling the fragrance. She handed him sugar, which he spooned into the pot, and two mugs which he filled with the pale, green-gold liquid.

And it will do you good. Donovan handed her the mug with a slight bow, as if it were a gift.

Good in what way? she asked, leading him back to the verandah.

In every way. This tea good for the head, good for the heart.

Yvonne threw back her head and laughed.

Is not lyrics, trust me. Ask anybody, ask Margie, she will tell you. Fevergrass cure for all kind of ache and pain.

Then it's just what I need, she said, raising the mug to her lips.

They sat silent for a while, sipping tea in the dark to a syncopated chorus of croaking lizards.

Tell me, Miss, Donovan suddenly asked, how come you leave America and come to live alone up here in this lonely old house, in this lifeless place?

Why do you want to know?

It seem strange…

I… I'm taking a break from New York, she said. I was… overworking. I needed a break. I can rest here. It's so peaceful, so beautiful. And hardly lifeless! Listen to the croakers! Look how everything grows so fast; it's uncontrollable!

That's not the kind of life I meant, he said. I wondering, where is your husband? He leaned closer and Yvonne caught the odour of sweat, damp earth, cut limes and decomposing leaves.

I don't have a husband.

What, a pretty lady like you with no husband? What's wrong with men in New York? He smiled, revealing large, yellowing teeth. She began to regret offering him tea.

I used to live with someone…

Ha, I knew…

We broke up over a year ago.

Oh, he said, looking grave. Then he nodded, as though all at once, he knew everything worth knowing about her. It rough when things mash up like that. Believe me, I know. Best make a fresh start… if you can, eh?

Yvonne didn't respond. In the silence that followed, the piercing song of a solo bird trilled above the hum of insect noises.

I use to live in town, in Kingston, Donovan announced suddenly. When I finish high school I moved to Kingston to work for my uncle. He own a lumber yard in Meadowfield and I go to learn the business from him.

Meadowfield! The place where they're having all that gang violence? I saw a report about it on the news just the other night. That must have been tough!

The violence wasn't so bad in those days. People had jobs, a young man could make a decent living. I stay by my uncle five years, learnin the business and savin money. My plan was to get away from Kingston, to come back here and start my own business. I wanted to be my own boss, and not work to make some other man rich.

He fell silent, gazing off into the dark.

So what happened to your plan? She scanned the wide set of his eyes, the curve of his jaw, as though these features could reveal whether a man was honest or a cheat.

He hesitated, then took a mouthful of tea.

Go on, she urged. You can't stop halfway through the story!

Well, he sighed. I come back and rent a small yard, a space near the market. I start tradin and business go well at first but then – you know how it goes. People mash up everythin. People takin things on credit and never payin. People stealin your goods when you're not lookin, your money when you not lookin. Before long the business crash and I in debt up to my eyes.

What do you do now?

Any work I can get. Yard work, farm work, any work… His mouth twisted in a bitter smile. There's no money here. A man can barely make a livin, barely feed his children. It can kill a man's soul.

Yvonne noticed the deep grooves on either side of his mouth, and realized he was older than she'd thought.

How old are your children? she asked, gently.

Ten and twelve. Two fine boys. They're in foreign, gone with their mother.

There was not enough light to read his expression.

Is five years now since I last saw them.

That must be hard…

Is a whole lot easier than havin them here and not havin food to give them.

So why didn't you go with them? She frowned. Was he a delinquent father, a negligent spouse?

I didn't have papers.

Then why doesn't their mother send them to visit you? Or why don't you go just for a visit?

He laughed and his teeth glistened in the dark.

Why don't I visit? He laughed again, a harsh sound. My wife send me money for the fare over a year ago. She send invitation, bank statement, everythin. I took everythin to the US Embassy, stand in line one whole day, fill out form, go back next day, go back the next week and what happen? No visa. Up till now, no visa.

Yvonne sank deeper into her chair, drawing back from his bitterness. She wished he would finish his tea and leave. She had enough sorrow of her own, she didn't need to share his.

Just last week I went back there and fill out new forms. I don't know why I bother, though. Is just a waste of time. But a man have to try, eh? He picked up his mug and drained it in one long quaff.

Is time I go home, he said, looking around for his shoes. I should finish up the back yard next Tuesday, easy. It will only take an hour or two more.

Yvonne got up to open the grille and switch on the verandah light so he could see his way out of the yard.

Within minutes of Donovan's departure, she heard the gate creak open.

Good evenin, good evenin! Margie's voice preceded her slender form up the garden path. Margie! Hey, girl!

Yvonne felt herself flushing, as if she had been caught misbehaving. She wondered how long Margie had been concealed in the yard.

Come on up, come take a seat!

I'm not sitting down for long. Donald soon come home for dinner, and I soon have to put the boys to bed. Margie flopped into the chair facing Yvonne. I see you met Donovan.

He says he knows you.

Margie crossed her slim legs. Her figure and face were youthful, almost girlish, in contrast to the thick, purplish veins curving across her calves, the legacy of three pregnancies.

Everybody here knows Donovan! He's a decent enough fellow... but I hear he love women too much.

Is there a man on this island who doesn't? Yvonne shrugged.

True... but he have a wife and some family problem... you know the kind of thing.

Actually, I don't.

What I'm trying to say is, you don't want to get too involved!

I'm not getting involved, I'm giving him work.

Maybe so, but... one thing can easily lead to another, eh? You didn't grow up around here; you wouldn't understand how a man like Donovan operates.

I don't understand what you're hinting at, Margie.

All I'm trying to tell you is, you have to be careful of people around here. Margie's voice dropped to a whisper. All of them looking for something, especially from somebody like you, coming from foreign.

What's *really* bothering you? The fact that he does manual work? That people around here will disapprove of me drinking tea with a yardman? Folks round here sure are backward!

I only mention it cause you're not... Margie faltered under her cousin's glare. Never mind. I done say what I come to say. Donald must be home by now, waiting for his dinner. I gone. She sprang to her feet, patted Yvonne's shoulder and hurried away, leaving her cousin fulminating at this fresh invasion of her privacy.

Around sundown on his third day in the yard, Donovan summoned Yvonne to inspect his handiwork.

You didn't know you had so much hiding under all that bush, eh? He had chopped back the croton hedge, pruned the bougainvillea and cut away the mango tree's overhanging branches. Yvonne trod gingerly over the spiky brownish crabgrass, making politely appreciative noises as Donovan pointed out a bed of stunted Easter lilies, the remains of a small rockery and, at the centre of the newly-made lawn, a cluster of straggly poinsettias.

Hmm. She looked around, not sure that she liked the yard now it was shorn of its lush overgrowth. I suppose it *is* a lot neater.

Donovan glanced at her face.

You miss the flowers, don't you? Don't worry, I'll make them bloom again for you.

That's quite a promise, Yvonne said, laughing.

Just a few hours a week, and you won't believe how everything will thrive!

I should have seen this coming.

Don't feel obliged –

Half a day, once a week, you say?

If you can afford it."

Oh… I suppose I can, she sighed. OK. She offered him her hand. "It's a deal.

He squeezed her hand in both his, thanking her repeatedly. She pulled away, embarrassed, saying it was nothing, really. She headed towards the back yard to see what changes he had made there.

On the afternoons he came to work, Yvonne sat on the verandah, tacking segments of dresses together or taking up hems. Sometimes when he was done, he rested on the step and they discussed the garden's progress. She discovered that Donovan was a mine of information about people in the village, most of whom he'd known since childhood. He was knowledgeable about the parish as a whole: its characters, its history, its places of danger, its beauty spots.

He must have sensed that Yvonne enjoyed his conversations, for he fell into the habit of stopping by just to wish her good day. Once, when she was out, he left a sack of jelly coconuts, husked and ready for piercing, propped up against the verandah door. Another time he left a bag of luscious, crimson otaheiti apples. The next time he arrived for work he was cradling a bunch of tiny apple bananas. He offered her the fruit with a small, solemn bow, and she warmed with pleasure at the delicacy of the gift.

One Friday morning as she was loading her dusty VW beetle in preparation for a trip into Kingston, Donovan appeared at her gate dressed in neatly pressed slacks and a short-sleeved white cotton shirt. He asked for a ride into town. He had an appointment at the US Embassy: more visa matters, he explained. Of course, she said, she could use some company on the road.

They climbed into the ancient car and set off on the road to Kingston. The road wound steeply into the valley, past acres of orderly banana groves, through dense emerald woods, levelling out alongside the glistening waters of a sweeping, sleepy river. The morning air retained a hint of the night's coolness, and though the sun was not yet high, its light played on the river's surface in a quivering, dazzling dance.

Do people here know how lucky they are, surrounded by all this beauty? Yvonne said.

Lucky? Donovan frowned. He had been deep in thought, as if inwardly rehearsing for the interview at the Embassy. Lucky? I call winning the Lotto lucky! Or getting through with a visa first time... He paused, looking wistful, contemplating the unlikely possibility of such luck passing his way. Then he shrugged and said:

There are places close to your house prettier than this. You ever swim at Strawberry Fields?

I haven't, but I'd like to, she said, thinking how seldom she went to the beach, how much she'd like to go someplace new. She felt Donovan's gaze on her face.

I need to see more of the island.

But you need company?

I guess so. She caught his glance for a second, then looked away.

Nothing more was said until they approached the outskirts of Kingston and hit a cloud of exhaust fumes from an unexpectedly long and sluggish line of traffic. All thought of beaches vanished from Yvonne's mind, replaced by the need to concentrate on the line of vehicles stretching as far as she could see.

Sunday morning, Donovan tapped on the verandah grille at eight o'clock. He wore a sky-blue shirt and beige polyester pants, a rolled-up towel under one arm, a bulging plastic bag in his hand.

Is a perfect morning for Strawberry Fields, he said as Yvonne unbolted the grille. What you think?

I'm sorry – I have a *pile* of work to do.

The day's perfect for the beach. The sun not too hot and the breeze just right. You could do your sewing this evening.

Yvonne fingered the strands of an unravelling braid. Then she laughed and threw up her hands. Yes! It *is* the perfect day! She hurried into the bedroom to rummage for a bathing suit.

Could she get away with a bikini? She pulled a favourite black two-piece from a drawer. Would he notice that one of her breasts was smaller than the other? She pulled on the bikini bra and scrutinized her reflection in the mirror, turning left, then right, and grunted, satisfied with what she saw. She pulled denim cut-offs and a white lawn shirt over the bikini, wrapped an Indian cotton scarf around her braids and stuffed sunscreen and oil into a Bloomingdale's beach bag, snatched her sunglasses from the dresser and hastened back to the verandah.

I have jelly coconuts. Donovan held up the plastic bag to show her.

But we need something to eat! Yvonne hurried to the kitchen, threw two mangos, two avocados and a packet of plain crackers into the beach bag, then hurried back to the verandah, ready.

As she started the VW, Margie's face popped up in Yvonne's head. The engine stalled. Should she be doing this? Then: Why not? *Why not?* She re-ignited the engine. What harm could come from an outing to the beach? She turned to flash a smile at Donovan, who settled back in his seat and strapped on his seat belt.

The road to the coast was punctuated with holes the size of trenches and sudden, sharp bends. Donovan attempted to start a conversation, but gave up, silenced by Yvonne's absorption in manoeuvring the car away from potholes. He spoke only to give her directions. They'd get to Strawberry Fields by a sharp turn off the main road, he explained, but the first turn they took led to the high, wrought-iron gates of a private house. The track was too narrow to turn; Yvonne had to reverse back to the main road.

Are you sure you know the way? If you're not, we should probably turn back.

Is only one wrong turn, Donovan said. You always give up so easy?

Yvonne bit her lip so as not to snap a sharp retort.

Anyway, there's the turn. Yes, that is it.

Yvonne was relieved to see a faded wooden sign pointing the way down a narrow turning, but as the aged car bumped and rattled along a seemingly endless, rock-strewn dirt track, what remained of her good spirits faded. By the time she pulled up under a clump of sea almonds, her head ached, her nerves were frazzled and she wished she were back on her verandah, alone. She stepped out of the beetle, slammed the door shut and leaned against it, trying to calm down. Donovan eased out of the car and reached into the back seat for their bags.

You look like you need a swim, he said, and frowned when Yvonne did not reply.

Yvonne followed behind as he led the way through a grove of sea pines to a tiny cove that was no more than a fringe of trees and a horseshoe of white sand embracing an expanse of sparkling azure water.

Tell me if you ever see any place as pretty as this, he said, with a proud gesture of his arm.

Yeah, it's pretty, she said offhandedly, and watched his face fall.

She spread her towel in the dappled shade of a palm tree, settled herself on the towel and began smoothing oil on her legs. Donovan spread his towel a cautious yard or so away. He sat fully clothed, knees drawn up, staring at the sea.

Their silence was disturbed by the sudden arrival of a

youth. He jogged out of nowhere and halted in front of Yvonne, one hand buried in the pocket of torn-off nylon sweatpants, the other outstretched, palm facing the sky.

Mornin, Miss, I'm hungry Miss, beg you a few dollars to buy breakfast?

Donovan jumped to his feet in a flurry of sand and lunged towards the boy, a stream of curses spewing from his mouth. The boy fled, disappearing through the trees.

Did you have to react like that? Yvonne jumped to her feet. Did you have to be so aggressive? The sudden, hostile outburst alarmed her: did he have a violent streak? Had he beaten his wife? Was that why she left him?

You don't understand these youths around here. Donovan kissed his teeth and sat again. They're good for nothin but beggin and stealin. Not one of them would consider doin a decent day's work for their money.

That's a bit harsh, isn't it? Yvonne loomed over him, hands on hips. Aren't you the one who's always saying how hard it is to survive around here, how there's no work, no money? She glared down at him. For a moment he glared back.

Besides, she continued, it's annoying when they beg, but it's not a crime. All they want is a few dollars. I don't mind handing out a few dollars now and then. It's the least I can do.

The least you can do?

Yes, the least I can do! To make up for having so much more than them.

He laughed at her, a hard, incredulous bark. Yvonne turned her back on him and strode towards the water, wondering what had possessed her to come to this deserted place with a man she barely knew, a man with nothing but disappointment to his name.

The morning sun was pale, but hot enough to bring a film of perspiration to her face. She removed her shorts and shirt and waded into the turquoise sea. Water brushed her skin like a cool caress as she strode in up to her waist. She scooped it up in cupped hands and rubbed her skin with it, like a balm. She lunged forward and swam breaststroke, pushing and kicking the water until she tired and paused to catch her breath. Only then did she think of Donovan sitting alone on the beach. She felt a surge of remorse. She stood up and turned to call out to him, but slipped on a large sea-stone and teetered backwards, and fell flat on the seabed.

When she surfaced, spluttering, she saw Donovan wading towards her, fully clothed. She beat the water with flailing arms and squeezed her eyes shut to ease the sting of salt. When she opened them, Donovan was beside her, lifting her. She let her head rest against his chest, feeling thankful. She breathed in the fresh-washed smell of his shirt and the deeper, earthy smell of his skin. Back on the sand, he put her down on the mat, but she held on to him and pulled him down beside her. He drew away with a quizzical frown, but she pulled him against her and he didn't resist. She kissed his face and he kissed her back, then she was tugging at his pants and wriggling out of her bikini with no thought of the symmetry of her breasts. They lay on the straw mat, her hands roaming his skin, her legs wrapped around him, holding him deep inside as they rocked and swayed to the rhythm of the waves.

They left the cove at sundown, driven away by swarms of spiteful sandflies. Back on the road, Yvonne took the narrow uphill bends with exaggerated turns of the steering wheel, whooping with glee as the beetle's tires screeched on the broken-up Tarmac, laughing at Donovan who strapped on his seat belt and urged her to take it slow. She let him out by the entrance to the lane that led to his tiny wooden house, one of a cluster of fragile-looking dwellings set back from the main road, behind a clump of trees. Less than half an hour later, he appeared at her door with a six-pack of Red Stripe. Together they foraged in Yvonne's refrigerator and found a bundle of callaloo, some onions and tomatoes which Donovan washed and chopped and set to cook in a large skillet, while Yvonne warmed a pot of rice left over from the previous day. They ate out on the verandah in the fading light, and afterwards sprawled in the two loungers, not talking much, sipping beer and tracking the moon's progress across the sky, until sun-drunk and love-weary, they fell into Yvonne's bed.

★

They had been lovers for a few weeks when Yvonne woke one morning, a dream fragment repeating in her head: Donovan striding down Seventh Avenue, smack in the middle of the road among buses, trucks and hooting cars, wearing a torn shirt, mud-smeared cut-offs, and down-at-heel, mashed-back shoes. She turned this fragment over and over. It was asking: Is there any future in this? She hadn't told him about her illness: what would he say when she did? What would he do? She sat up in bed and scanned his face on the pillow by her side. He slept on his back, one arm dangling over the bed's edge. He frowned in his sleep, and his lips twitched as though engaged in a silent debate. Yvonne threw back the sheet that covered him, exposing the soft mound of his genitals, and long, sinewy legs. Skin the colour and texture of bark, and across the shins a network of shiny, satin scars, upfront and visible, not concealed by discreet folds of skin, like hers. His skin told a story of labour and toil; hers tucked its it sorrows neatly away.

So, you think you get a good bargain? Donovan was watching her through bleary eyes.

Bargain? She drew up the sheet and snuggled against his side. I pay for your labour, not your body, she said.

Yard work, bed work, it's one and the same, he said, pulling her close.

You can't mean that! She slid over him.

Well, this kind is sweeter, he acknowledged, reaching his arms around her.

And this kind is free, she added, touching her mouth to his.

When more weeks passed without even one visit from Margie, Yvonne concluded that her cousin knew Donovan was sleeping over and did not approve. She suspected that the entire community was gossiping, but she was too happy to let such narrow-mindedness worry her. How did Donovan feel? He belonged here, he knew these people, he was a married man, even though his wife had been absent for years. Did he mind his private life being public knowledge? She raised the matter with him over a Sunday morning breakfast.

People will talk, yes. What you expect? He shrugged, more concerned with piling ackees and green bananas onto his plate. Then he said: Listen, Yvonne. You remember the time we went to Kingston? You remember I went to the embassy to reapply for a visa? Well, the papers come through! I get the visa!

She reached across the table to squeeze his hand. Honey, I'm glad for you. When did you hear?

A few days ago.

And you never mentioned it?

I never said anything because... well because... He sighed and set down his fork. He put his elbows on the table and dropped his head on his hands.

Because of what?

Because I don't know if I can go.

What do you mean? I don't understand you. You have the visa, you have the money for your ticket...

The money I have is not enough, he said, raising his head. It not enough. I have it over a year now and I spend some of it. I need two hundred US more to make up the fare. His voice faded to a whisper. Can you lend it to me?

A cold mass settled on Yvonne's shoulders. She sat still in her chair.

So here it is, she said eventually. So that's what all the tea-drinking was about. And the otaheiti apples. And Strawberry Fields...

I never plan for this to happen, Yvonne, believe me! He reached across the table for her hands, which she pulled away and buried between her knees. If you can help me, if you can lend me the money, I'll pay you back.

How, Donovan? How could you pay me back on the pittance you earn? How do you even know I have the money to lend you? Yvonne was on her feet, shouting.

You come from foreign, don't you? And you've been flinging your money away on beggars... His voice trailed off. Suddenly his brows snapped together. You mean, you don't have the money...?

Yvonne stared at him across the table. His posture, slightly hunched and pleading, was a cliché, a banal picture of neediness. She felt no sympathy at all.

Donovan, she said, what happened to your pride?

She stood and turned her back on him. She strode into the bedroom, snapping the door shut behind her. She was trembling, though the morning was hot. She climbed into bed fully clothed, drew her knees up and wrapped her arms around them, but the trembling would not stop.

She fell into a shallow sleep and woke to a feeling of warmth, as if Donovan's body was stretched spoon-like against her back, his arm thrown across her waist, the way they always slept. She turned to touch him and touched instead a vacant space. She jumped out of bed, heart pumping. There was no sign of him in the living room or in the kitchen. Breakfast was still on the table, his food abandoned, her own plate empty. Her belly gripped with a pain sharper than hunger. Tears stung her eyes.

She began to search for her pocket book, almost in a panic, and found it in its usual place in a corner of the bedroom. She fumbled for her chequebook and a pen. Dropping on the bed, she wrote a cheque for two hundred dollars, then crossed out the two and replaced it with a three, breathing a loud sigh of relief as she searched for an envelope. She pulled on a pair of sandals and hurried out of the house, heading towards the lane where Donovan lived. She half-ran down the road, oblivious of the heat burning down on her head. She wasn't sure which of the small dwellings clustered along the dusty track was his and asked a boy passing her on a rusted bicycle if he knew Donovan. The boy pointed to a neat-looking house fringed with white and red hibiscus.

She knocked on the unvarnished wooden door, but there was no answer, so she bent and pushed the envelope underneath. She imagined his delight at opening the envelope and seeing the cheque. Straightening up, she felt a surge of happiness, imagining him smiling with relief. She wouldn't linger, she would hurry back home since she still had work to do on the bridesmaids' dresses for the politician's daughter's wedding. She would keep busy until Donovan came by.

He must have jumped over the garden gate while she was at the sewing machine because she didn't hear the gate creak open. He must have crept up the path to the verandah. He must have pushed the envelope hard under the verandah grille, for it lodged against a chair leg, insignificant and crumpled as a discarded tissue. She found it at sundown when she'd gone outside to sit and wait, not knowing he had come and gone.

PEOPLE FOR LUNCH

Through her kitchen window Corinne watched a grey wall of rain approach from the summit of Jack's Hill. It would reach Barbican in a few seconds. It would splash down in thunderous torrents and turn her garden into a swamp. Damn, damn! She hated the way the weather would suddenly change and ruin her plans. As she beat the bundle of callaloo she had just rinsed against the side of the sink to dry it, she wondered for the hundredth time why she had to live in a place where the weather was unpredictable, and where she couldn't buy frozen, ready-washed greens.

The rain meant she would not be able to serve lunch out in the garden under the mango trees; it meant that good money had been wasted hiring the pretty wrought-iron tables and chairs that cluttered the lawn, waiting for Winston to arrange them. Well, they would be useless now. Lunch would have to be served indoors, never mind there wasn't quite enough seating space for all the guests. Corinne toyed with the idea of calling Petra to complain about this setback, then decided against it. Petra was bringing the guest of honour, but since the lunch party and the house were hers, she would figure out what to do.

How much easier life would be if she lived in Miami, like her sister Lynette. Everything one needed could be bought cheaply there; foods of every kind at the super-market, making for one-stop shopping. No need to stop at the fish market, then at the market for vegetables, and then the dry goods store. No need to wash and shred bundle after bundle of callaloo. If Winston were to turn to her in bed one night and say, *Sweetness, how would you like to get off this island for a year or two?* It would make her life. Yes, it would. Oh, it was true that Winston had given her everything a woman could reasonably want. They owned a comfortable house in a quiet, gated community in Barbican, where the other residents were also profes-sionals, bankers like Winston, lawyers and businessmen and their families. He had bought her a new BMW SUV for her birthday, and he gave her an ample budget to keep the house running smoothly. And they had Pierre, her beautiful baby boy. But she wanted more *quality* in her life. She loved to plan lunches and dinners, weekend trips to the country, Sunday trips to the beach; *nice things*, that brought people together to have a good time. She liked to plan in detail and, most of all, she liked to make those plans happen just as she imagined them. It was the unpredictability of everything – the weather, the people, the economy – that made planning even the smallest thing a waste of time.

And where was Winston? Hadn't she told him she needed his help with some basic but important things like moving the furniture around? Where was he? If it weren't for the rain, the sun would be hot, high in the sky, and he was upstairs in bed, his lanky limbs sprawled out, fast asleep, and probably snoring. Earlier, as she had got out of bed to answer Pierre's hungry screams, she had nudged Winston sharply in the back saying, Hey, you! Get up and help me prepare for this party instead of sleeping till the sun gets hot. Surprise me for once!

He had opened one gummy, weary eye and then rolled over, remembering, in a sleepy haze, what it felt like to sleep long and late without interruption and without guilt. Wouldn't a reasonable woman let him rest? Wouldn't a reasonable woman feel he did his share? He had put in sixty-five hours at the bank over the previous six days. He gave Corinne enough money to get the help she needed. He had pulled the top sheet over his balding head and settled down to a few more hours of sleep.

Mid-morning found Corinne still figuring out where to serve lunch, while she washed lettuce and kept a distracted eye on Pierre who was noisily crashing around the open-plan kitchen in his Miami-bought babywalker. Where was Icilyn when she needed her to take Pierre off her hands? As to where to serve lunch, there was the dining room, of course, but twenty hungry guests milling around a buffet table would crowd the small room. There was the verandah: fully grilled and decorated with a lush array of palms, and just spacious enough to accommodate twenty. She could set up a buffet out there, but if the wind blew high, rain would come in. It wouldn't do to have the guest of honour, Eduardo Matista, the great Cuban choreographer, eating lunch off his lap amid squalls of rain. Corinne's face puckered, as though she had bitten into an unexpectedly sour plum. It would have to be the dining room, which meant that when that wretch Icilyn deigned to turn up, she would have to dust it down, first thing. Problem solved. Corinne smoothed back her bobbed hair, sighed with relief and returned to washing lettuce.

At that moment Icilyn crept in through the verandah door, wet and flustered. Drops of rain clung to her greying hair, and water seeped from her black sneakers.

Sorry I'm late, Mrs Winters, she said, quickly slipping off the sneakers and walking barefoot into the kitchen. Her face was lined and tired-looking. Her eyes creased at the corners in contrition. Shakila, my youngest, she sick with fever this morning. Lord knows what's wrong with her, and then the bus took forever…

Something always happens to make you late, eh? Corinne's tone was intended as light but it came out sharp. Icilyn had been with her for five years and wasn't a bad worker, but she lived way up in the hills near Mavis Bank and was often late. She always came with some excuse: the bus didn't arrive, or the bus broke down, or she couldn't get on the bus it was so crammed. Not even good excuses. Corinne would have fired her a long while ago, but she didn't have the heart to fire a single mother who was struggling to raise three children.

Never mind that now, Corinne continued. Hurry up and change out of those wet clothes. I need you to dust down the dining room right away. And when you've finished, I want you to come and fix the fish. Oh, and when Mr Winters gets up, you can straighten the bedroom. And take Pierre with you.

Corinne returned to her preparations.

Lord, there's so much to do!

A glassy-eyed Icilyn picked up the now fractious Pierre and hurried away to change her clothes with the child balanced on her hip.

The lunch had been Petra's idea. She was Corinne's oldest friend and Pierre's godmother. She was the director of the Kingston Academy of Dance, where the world-renowned Cuban maestro was the guest instructor for the summer. Getting the maestro to teach at the Academy's summer school had been quite a coup, a feather which Corinne, the Chair of the management committee, had helped to put in Petra's cap. Corinne took her responsibilities seriously. She was the one who'd suggested bringing someone from overseas. She was the one who'd raised the funds to pay the Maestro's fee, with some help from Winston, but only a little. Petra, who had no interest in fundraising, had been thrilled and grateful. Now she could show those snotty, would-be patrons of the arts from uptown what poor little Petra from Paradise View could pull in. Well, Corinne planned to do a little showing off of her own, with fabulous cocktails, delicious food and an array of affluent, influential guests.

In truth, Petra should have given the party herself, but her house was too far out of town, it was small, had no verandah and no air-conditioning. Why she chose to live out in Paradise View in the shoebox she'd inherited from her mother was beyond Corinne's understanding. She should have sold it and invested the money in an apartment somewhere central, like Barbican, or quiet like Hope Pastures. Corinne and Petra had both grown up in Paradise View. Corinne's family had moved there from the country when she was a child. At that time, those little three-bedroomed houses, with their small patches of backyard and tiny porches, had really seemed like paradise. Now she looked back in embarrassment at the bliss she felt the first time she turned on a faucet and saw running water, the first time she switched on an electric light, or used a flushing indoor toilet. And the joy of not having to fetch water before school in the mornings! As the elder of two girls, that task had been hers when they lived in the hills of St Catherine. As long as she lived she would never forget that daily ordeal: a three-hundred-yard trek from the village standpipe to the old house, her carrying-arm straining at her shoulder socket, and water slopping out of the enamel pail onto the red dirt, making mud around her feet.

She and Petra, who had lived just across the street, had won scholarships to the Maria Immaculata Convent High School in Kingston. Every weekday morning they had set out together, marching side by side to catch the bus to town, Corinne, fresh-faced and clear skinned, with thick plaits resting on her shoulders; Petra, small, skinny and dark. They hurried down the road to the bus stop, proudly dressed in identical starched white poplin uniforms, belted with sashes the deep colour of the morning sky. Every afternoon they would return home, tired from the crowded bus ride, thirsty from the chalky dust that blew off the road to Paradise View, and hungry for the meals they would have to start preparing until their mothers came home from work.

Petra had been a Saturday morning dancer. She took classes in classical ballet and modern technique and excelled at both. Corinne had shared in Petra's pride and jubilance when she won a scholarship to the Royal Ballet School in London, whisking it from under the tender feet of those sepia girls from Stony Hill, Cherry Gardens and Arcadia. The whole community of Paradise View had attended the send-off party Petra's parents had thrown for her. When she returned after eight years in England, with plans to start a school of her own in Kingston, the community crowded into her parents' house to celebrate her safe return.

Corinne had graduated from Maria Immaculata with the second highest grades in her class. These earned her a secretarial job at the headquarters of the island's largest bank, a position she soon vacated to become a teller. While Petra was away in London, Corinne progressed determinedly through the bank's hierarchy to arrive at the position of assistant manager in charge of small loans. By the time her old friend returned home with plans to open a dancing school, Corinne was able to advise her on who to talk to about finding premises, and where to look for funding. She, Corinne, had laid the foundation for Petra's success. Petra didn't know who was who in Kingston, didn't understand business, or the way money circulated on the island. How could she, coming from England via Paradise View? Corinne's life path, on the other hand, had followed the pattern foretold for Maria Immaculata girls: that of secretary or wife to an uptown man. Corinne achieved the first goal and transcended it. She achieved the second by marrying her boss.

By midday Corinne felt she could relax. The wooden floor of the living room shone, the cushions on the two large sofas had been plumped, the knickknacks scattered on the side-tables were all properly dusted. The dining room table was spread with her best lace cloth and laid with mats and cutlery, just waiting for the dishes of food: crab and avocado salad; snapper stuffed with callaloo and baked in a peppery tomato sauce; scalloped potatoes, a vegetable medley, and her special tipsy pudding for desert. Corinne's mouth watered. Petra had suggested serving curry goat and green bananas, with sweet potato pudding for desert.

Why not serve a traditional meal? she'd said. Why not give the Maestro a taste of traditional Jamaican cooking? Poor Petra. Didn't she know that men like Mike Leonard, the Chair of Raven Merchant Bank, and Richard Best, from Standard Investments did not eat such food. Who ate green bananas these days? Certainly not she, Corinne Winters, even though Winston was always asking for them. He liked them for breakfast, with salt herrings. As a child she had consumed enough green bananas for a lifetime. From infancy until she left home, green bananas as porridge, as dumplings, as boiled, as fried, as mashed. From she could reach the kitchen sink it had been her task to peel them and no complaints, or she'd get a sharp slap from her mother. The thick, fibrous skins had torn her thumbnails and left stains on her fingers that took years to wash off. Even then, back in Paradise View, green bananas had been ashes in her mouth, the taste of poverty on her tongue.

Her thoughts were interrupted by Winston, who had dressed and eaten a late breakfast, and was reclining on the verandah reading *The Sunday Gleaner*.

Corinne, he shouted, come see this! It looks like Raven Merchant Bank is in serious trouble!

Not right now, Winston, she replied, but at the back of her mind she was thinking: Oh no. Not another one. She had stopped reading newspapers. Why fill up your head with bad news? Weren't there enough bad things happening around them, all the time, every day? The TV news was almost as bad. Nothing but murders, armed robberies, businesses going bust, banks collapsing. Last year, the People's Bank had crashed and its Chairman, their neighbour, Alex Richards, had lost everything. House, cars, boat, everything. Overnight. Just the other day Corinne had seen poor Cynthia Richards walking down Hope Road in the hot sun, a pair of worn-out sandals on her feet and a shopping bag in her hand, looking like a domestic helper for the whole world to see. As she drove past, Corinne had felt fear stir in her belly. How dreadful, she whispered as she rolled up the car window.

She inspected the lounge and the dining room one last

time, and fussed about on the verandah, clearing away the discarded sections of Winston's paper. He was engrossed in the finance section; all she could see of him were two long, hairy legs and feet clad in black flip-flops.

Why don't you put on those blue slacks I bought you, she said. He could look so elegant when he dressed properly. Winston lowered the paper for just a second to peer at her.

I like these shorts. They're comfortable. He returned his attention to the paper.

Corinne gave up and went upstairs to get ready. Icilyn had ironed her white linen pants-suit, so all she had left to do was shower and dress. Icilyn was in the kitchen putting the salads together and then she was going to bathe Pierre and dress him in the cute denim outfit she had bought on her last Miami shopping spree. As she lathered her body in the shower, Corinne hummed a tune in pleasure.

When the doorbell rang, it startled her. She thought it was Petra arriving early with the Maestro, so she shouted down to Icilyn to open the door. She was surprised when Icilyn tapped on the bedroom door and whispered, Mrs Winters, your guests are arriving. She thought she had timed everything perfectly and felt more than a little fazed, but she hurried downstairs to greet the Bests, hand extended, smile warm. From then onwards, the doorbell kept ringing and soon the living room was filled with the hum of chatter and clusters of men and women with drinks in their hands, but no Petra and no Maestro. How like Petra to stage an entrance that would make her the centre of attention.

They were the last to arrive by a good half-hour. Petra swept into the lounge, slender and graceful in a flowing red dress, with a wide, happy smile, pleased with the effect of her late entrance. She entered on the arm of the Maestro, who was built like a god and had the chiselled face of an ebony carving. He was dressed in white and wore a wide-brimmed Panama hat, which gave him an elegant, romantic air. He progressed slowly through the room, listening politely as Petra introduced him, shaking hands with each of the guests. He spoke very little English, which disconcerted Corinne. Why had she not prepared a greeting in Spanish? When he had met everyone he sat on one of the sofas and crossed his legs. Petra sat beside him, beaming, as though aware of their beauty and pleased with the picture they made.

Corinne had no time to appreciate the picture: she was ready to put out the food, but where was Icilyn? She looked round for Winston. If he was the slightest bit of use, he'd be helping her now, but he was in a corner, head-to-head with Richard Best, no doubt discussing the problems at Richard's bank.

She shouted upstairs, Icy, where are you? I need you right now!

Icilyn called back, I'm coming, Mrs Winter, I'm on the phone with Erica, my eldest, she says Shakila...

You're on the phone? Get down here right now! Corinne rushed to the kitchen to dish out the crab and avocado salad and arrange bread rolls in a basket.

Icilyn appeared beside her, breathless. It's Shakila, Mrs Winters, Erica says...

Never mind that now, you fool! Get the food on the table! Corinne dashed out of the kitchen with the crab salad and rolls, and did not see the flare in Icilyn's eyes. On the way to the dining room she glimpsed Pierre scampering amid the guests, naked. She blinked and he was gone. She dismissed the image from her mind. Heading back to the dining room to set more dishes on the table, she saw the Maestro lift Pierre onto his lap, and heard him say: *Nino, dondé estan tus pantalones?*

Icilyn! roared Corinne, past caring who heard. Get my child out of there at once!

At that moment Pierre, with perfect aim and timing, released a stream of urine onto the Maestro's crotch. Corinne froze, speechless. Petra leaped from the sofa and ran to the kitchen to look for paper towels and Icilyn. Icilyn was pulling on her sneakers. Ignoring Petra, she marched through the living room and out through the front door.

You mark my words, said Corinne to the person standing nearest, *by this time next year I'll be gone from here.* The person was Mrs Richard Best, who reached out and touched Corinne's arm with a sympathetic murmur.

Winston, sensing a crisis, emerged from the corner where he and Richard Best had been ensconced. He rose to the occasion, to everyone's surprise. He took hold of Pierre and the distraught Maestro, and led them upstairs to find some trousers.

TEN DAYS IN JAMAICA

From I was a dusty-knee boy in short pants going to elementary school, Granny has been telling me how man born to suffer. *Baltimore, this life is a vale of tears,* Granny been singing in my ears these nineteen years, day in, day out. She with her face all wrinkle, hair all grey, body all bent up. You can tell just by looking that her life has been just that. A vale of tears.

Lord knows, it has been hard for her, raising me and my little sister Binta when she was already an old lady. My mother, she pack up and go to foreign nine years ago now, when Binta was a tot and I was ten. Granny say she went to find work so she could save money and send for Binta and me. She went to make a start at building a good life for us in New York. Well, I hear she's doing well over there. Whenever she remember, she send a few dollars, just enough to buy clothes and pay school fees, but not enough to buy school books, or pay for doctor when me or Binta get sick. And Binta get sick often; she was so skinny, her legs long and thin like broomsticks, you could tell her constitution wasn't strong. The two of us used to catch cold when it rained and the bedsheet get damp and our shoes grow mildew. We was often sick, and hungry too, when we was small.

Yes, Granny did struggle hard with us. She's strict as a schoolteacher and provoking as hell sometimes, but I don't know how Binta and me would have managed without her. After Mama left, we had nothing. Those were the days we ate cornmeal for breakfast, dinner and supper. But Granny stay positive. *Baltimore*, Granny use to say to me, *is only God help your mother get a visa so she could get to New York. One day, God willing, she will send for you. Give thanks and praises.*

Three years ago at Christmas, Binta catch a cold that turn to bronchitis and then turn to pneumonia. Granny was so worried about Binta that she send me over to Miss Zelda's place to phone my mother – Granny didn't have a phone at that time. I had to tell Mama that Binta was sick, that it was serious and she must come as soon as she could. At first, when I hear my mother's voice at the end of the line I didn't know who I was talking to. It sound like someone strange, a lady with an American accent who kept asking, *Is that you, Baltimore?* I said, *Yes Mama, it's me*, for though she sounded strange, I realize it was Mama. But then I didn't know what else to say.

She tell me she going to send money by Western Union for medicine for Binta. She tell me to call her if Binta get any worse. Well, Binta get better, but she was weak and she get so skinny, a strong breeze could blow her over. Granny went over to Miss Zelda herself and call our mother to talk about Binta. Granny didn't tell me what she said to Mama, but within a week Mama send letter and bank statement and money to get visa and airplane ticket so Binta could fly to New York to be with her. Granny pay Mr Sam, our nearest neighbour, to drive her and Binta to Kingston to the American Embassy. They lucky; they get the visa first time.

When Mr Sam drove Granny, Binta and me to MoBay to put Binta on the plane to New York, Binta cry the whole journey like she didn't want to leave. I wanted to tell her not to be so fool, that she should be glad she get the chance to leave, but I didn't have the heart. At the departure gate she hug me tight and I couldn't stop the water that well in my eyes. Even Granny was dabbing her eye-corners with a handkerchief. My heart was hurting the whole time we waited in the car park to watch Binta's plane take off, hurting because my baby sister was leaving, and hurting because I had to stay.

★

So when Chips called me on the phone and said: *Suzy, how about ten days in Jamaica? I've found a steal deal!* I didn't even blink. I said, *Yeah, girl, you're on*. Chips (her real name is Christine), gushed down the phone. *You'll love Jamaica*. She breathed like she was talking about her latest crush; like I even needed to be persuaded. *Branscombe Bay is like a postcard: all white sand beaches and palm trees swaying in the wind. When you're there, you won't want to come back to London*.

It sounded great from where I was sitting, in the data processing room where I work with eight other girls. The job pays well, but it's as boring as hell. It was more fun when Chips used to work here. We used to have a lot of laughs then. But right now it's pretty grim. On a wintry day like today the dingy windows and the feeble grey daylight are enough to depress you, never mind the stinging cold outside. I said to Chips, *Yeah, you're on*. Then I picked up the phone to call home and tell my Mum.

Jamaica? she said. *What do you want to go there for? What's wrong with Spain?* Spain was my Mum's favourite holiday place.

What's the food going to be like? And can you trust the

57

hotels over there? My mum and dad had bought into a timeshare, a villa in a tourist development just outside Marbella. They went over there twice a year, for three weeks in the summer and a week at New Year, regular as clockwork

At least you know what you're going to get in Spain. Those were Mum's last words on the matter, at least, the last words I was going to entertain. I quickly said goodbye and hung up, then went straight away to the supervisor's office to book my leave.

★

The day my mother left, I did cry a whole bucket of eyewater. I remember running after the taxi that was taking her to Montego Bay to catch the plane, bawling after her, and she, hanging out of the window was bawling too. I was small, but when Granny explain Mama was going away to a money place, a place where man didn't have to work ground or cut banana or chop cane to make a living, I understand why she left us. I even understand why she send for Binta, who write me often and tell me she's putting on weigh and doing well in her new school. She say she settle down quite nice in Brooklyn. She say Mama got a good job and they are living comfortable as anything. But since the day I talk to her on the phone about Binta, I haven't heard from my mother. Up till now I can't understand why in all those years, she never send for me, her first-born child, nor even came back to Jamaica to look for me.

The best thing Granny ever did was use some of the likkle money Mama send to buy some bamboo and zinc and build a restaurant at the front of her house. Nothing fancy, just a space big enough for three tables and a bar.

58

I was about twelve at the time, but I paint the doorway a bright shade of blue and paint a sign to hang over the doorway: **MISS ROSIE'S JERK JOINT**. I beg two hibiscus suckers from Miss Zelda and plant one on either side of the door to pretty-up the place: to make it look decent and attractive so tourist would stop and spend money.

When the restaurant open, I help Granny after school, serving the food she cook. From the very first day the restaurant open, people in the community came to eat. The tourists took their time to come, but word spread down to Branscombe, and one by one they start to come up the hill in their rented cars. Once they start coming, Granny never fool around, she raise her prices. The people in the community couldn't afford our food after that, but I never mind, cause if Granny never raise more money I would have never finish school, and Binta would have never get to go to school at all.

*

After seven hours in an airplane I was limp with fatigue, but I switched on like a light once I stepped out of the plane into the warm sun. Montego Bay! I felt like I already knew the place, from TV ads and travel brochures and songs on my Gran's *Best of Harry Belafonte* CD. The bus from our hotel took off down a road following the coast. I don't think I'd ever seen sea this blue before. I hung out of the window, like an excited kid, breathing in the tangy, fruity air. Chips sat beside me, staring out with a gleam in her eyes, like a retriever who's spotted a bone and can't wait to go get it. She was all made up, lips glossy, every hair on her frosted blonde head gelled in place. The skin exposed by the skimpy

59

halter-top she was wearing was already light gold, from fake tanner.

And what are you staring at? she said, catching me looking at her. At your chest, I said looking pointedly at her breasts jiggling underneath a light cotton jersey top. Chips was twig thin, apart from her boobs. I'm dressed for the climate, she said breezily. When are you going to get out of those things? Or are you going to walk round Branscombe Bay dressed like the Virgin Mary? She tugged at my cotton shirt like she wanted to pull it off me. She says I have no dress sense, that I dress like my Mum. But I give her back as good as I get. I've told her countless times that she looks like a sixties tart with those micro skirts she wears and those clunky shoes and ice pink lips. She just laughs and tells me to fuck off. She thinks she looks sexy.

As the bus entered a quaint little town, all narrow streets and higglety-pigglety houses, the driver's voice came booming through the tannoy: Welcome to Branscome Bay. This charming town has many interesting shops, galleries and historic buildings. Its many restaurants are well worth a visit. A short drive out of the town takes you into our exquisite countryside. Our desk staff will be happy to assist you with car hire.

Oooh, I said, we should do that one day. Chips, smirks like she had a wicked, secret plan. You can, if you want. I'll have better things to do. I wanted to be let in on the secret, but she looked away, not answering, but still smirking.

By the time we arrived at the hotel it was dark, but still very warm. At the reception desk a girl in a blue uniform with a pink flower in her hair shook my hand and welcomed us to Jamaica in a lilting voice. Told us her name was Jackie and she was here to help us.

I wanted to ask about hiring a car but Chips dragged me away. I followed her out of the reception area and down a winding path lit up with fairy lights to a cluster of painted wooden cottages set back from the path.

This one is ours, Chips said, unlocking the door of a tiny, pale peach cottage. Inside was a large room with two single beds, two chairs and a dressing table. A gleaming white-tiled bathroom led off to one side. At the back was a small verandah furnished with a two-seater wicker sofa, two armchairs, and a small, glass topped wicker table. It was all very tasteful, very nice. Chips threw her suitcase on the bed and began unpacking, not even pausing for a breather.

C'mon, she said, don't just stand there gawping at me. Let's get dressed and get out! So saying, she flounced off into the bathroom, toilet bag in hand, leaving me to unpack my things and decide what to wear.

★

The restaurant bring in money, but Granny hold on to what she get like a hungry dog with a bone. She give me two hundred Jamaican weekend time: as though a man can do anything with two hundred dollars! Just the other day I get vex when she hand me the two greasy bills. I tell her the money she give me not enough. She puff out her chest like a croaking lizard and say: *What a young boy like you doing with big money when you not paying rent nor buying food?* I tell you, it was hard to remember my manners. I could have cuss two bad word in her ears, but instead I remind her that I'm nearly twenty. I leave school three years ago; I'm not a boy any more.

Still, I have my own way of making a few extra bills. Those girls that stop by here now and again… Well, I never wanted to fool around with them at first, though from they started coming to the cafe I get plenty of invitation to go down to Branscombe, to take them out dancing, out to bars, down to the beach at night. I never want to go with them at first but plenty of the man round here do it. And since we don't have electricity yet, Granny shut the cafe at nightfall, so I have plenty time to kill at nights. So I tell myself that nothing wrong with it: I'm not thieving or anything. These women, all they want is a little company, a little sweetness. And not all of them want to sex me, but if that's what they want, it not so hard to oblige, if the price is right. Tell you the truth, it not hard at all. Especially when I get a nice one with plenty of money, one who will buy me a shirt or a nice pants, so I look good when I go out with her. And when she leave, she will put money in my hand. Ten pounds, twenty US, thirty euros. And if I really did good, fifty, or even a hundred.

An Italian woman give me two hundred US after I spend two night with her. A big old married woman, with diamond ring and gold band on her finger. She lock me up in her hotel room and we drink champagne nonstop those two nights and the whole day in between. Boy, I work hard for that money. You can't imagine how. But I was able to retire for a couple weeks with the money she give me. I did consider using it to buy a little drinks cart, cause I know the vendors down by the beach do quite well. Miss Zelda's husband, Stanley, use to sell ice cream down in Branscombe. He did good business, enough to give Miss Zelda comfortable home, with electricity and phone. But one night, when he was wheeling his cart home, some bad men set on him. I heard that they beat him first, thief all his takings and when he was lying in the road, one of them pull out a gun and bam! shoot him dead. So I consider buying a cart, but when I remember what happen to Stanley I said chuh! Who want to spend their days burning up under hot sun to make gunman rich? Not me.

★

After one week in Branscombe Bay I was well into life in the tropics. I forgot about London, forgot about the DP room. In the mornings I had breakfast on the verandah and watched hummingbirds darting in and out of flowers. After breakfast I'd go down to the beach, but it was a job getting Chips out of bed to come with me. We'd had words after our first night. We'd gone out to this club by the waterside and what did she do? She picks up this Rasta and brings him back to the hotel! Next morning she tried to explain that it wasn't the way it looked, that she'd met the guy Silver on her last trip to Jamaica. Well, I don't know what she and him were doing out there on the verandah, but I told her plain, if she wanted to bonk, she either had to do it when I wasn't around, or do it some place else. She went all bitchy on me then. *Who do you think you are, telling me how to behave? If you weren't such an old maid you'd be bonking yourself, and enjoying it!* Who's she calling an old maid? I'm only twenty-three! Well, I didn't speak to her that whole day, but you can't keep ignoring someone you're on holiday with for long, can you?

Anyhow, when she's with Silver, her Rasta friend, I hang out with some of the other guests at the poolside bar. I made friends with Lisbet and Franke, two German girls who spent all day by the pool toasting themselves to a crisp.

Where's your friend, Lisbet asked me once, is she with

63

her rental? Her rental? I said, thinking of hired cars. Her, er, boyfriend. My face burned all of a sudden. It's nothing to be ashamed of! Lisbeth giggled. They're part of the local attractions, no? It's what we come here for – a little sun, a little smoke, a little romance.

I didn't know about the romance part, nor the smoke either. I couldn't see myself hooking up with a local. Not that I haven't had the chance. I was down by the beach sitting at a bar on my own one afternoon when this local fella sits beside me and starts giving me the eye. He wasn't bad looking at all, but I kept right on sipping my pina colada and reading my book. I hoped he would take the hint and go away.

Your friend gone and left you alone? I ignored him, but he kept trying. A nice lady like you shouldn't be drinking on your own. I shifted on the bar stool so my back was almost turned on him. My friend will be here soon. He laughed and as I turned to look at him I noticed white teeth with a gap in the front, lush eyelashes and long, long dreadlocks. He was quite nice looking, really, and he was no more than twenty. Your friend getting a little sweetness, he said. Now he was really getting on my nerves. How would he know? He flashed me a seductive smile. Her friend Silver's my bredrin. I know he's taking good care of her. You should let me take care of you, baby, he drawled. I was ready for him. Don't "baby" me! I'm not American and neither are you! He eased off the bar stool. Relax, baby, ease up a bit. How would a foreign lady like you understand me if I didn't twang a little? He strolled off, leaving me with my drink and my bodice-ripper novel for company.

★

One evening a couple years back I was sweeping out the restaurant, getting ready to lock up. I heard a car pull up outside and I know from the way the engine run smooth it was a rental. I was getting ready to announce that we finished serving for the day, but when the man step inside, I couldn't say the words. He look like some kind of movie star. Tall and suntan, face not shaved, hair spike-up; he resemble Clint Eastwood when he was young. He sat down at a table and watched me scraping up the dust, with a look in his eye I didn't like.

Do you have a cold beer? He didn't sound American or English: I couldn't tell where he was from. I wasn't spending too much time with tourists in those days: I wasn't so familiar with their different accents. I gave him a Red Stripe and waited behind the bar till he finish. He was staring at me hard, but I pretend not to notice. I pretend to listen to the radio.

He swallowed the beer fast and came across to the bar. I need someone like you to show me around here, he said, plain and matter of fact, like he was ordering food. I pay very well. Then he showed his teeth in a hard-man kind of smile.

I have to tell you the truth, I didn't know what to say. I started to stammer some rubbish or other while he stood there watching me like a mongoose staring down a mouse. Just then, Granny came in through the back door, wiping her hands on her apron. I already told you Granny was no fool. She stood by the door and stare at the man hard. Then she started to talk, not to me, not to the man, but loud, and she was quoting the Bible.

Revelations chapter three, verse eleven, she said, like she was getting ready to preach. She wasn't looking at anyone in particular but the man just stood up and straighten-up himself, turned on his heel and walked off.

Well, I know plenty of man round here wouldn't have said no to that man, but me, I'm not going that far. It would have to be one whole heap of money to get me with a man. A whole heap. And even then, I don't think so. One thing I already learn is that sometimes the money don't really cover the cost. Like the one time I get capture by a wrinkle-up old French woman. When I walk into her hotel beside her, the staff stare at us so hard I feel shame. Then again, sometimes the money don't matter so much. If the girl is cute, if she smile nice at me, I don't mind giving her time, even if she don't have money. Tell you the truth, that is when I really don't mind the escort business.

★

I don't understand why Chips invited me to come on holiday with her, I really don't. She rolls up in the early hours of the morning, drunk or stoned and smelling like frowsty underwear, then she sleeps until late afternoon. All that talk about white sand beaches and palm trees. God knows where she goes with that Silver, but I don't think she's spent more than two hours on a beach and even less time with me.

I'd been seeing more and more of Lisbeth and Franke, but now Lisbet's hooked up with a Shaggy look-alike, leaving me and Franke to make the best of the fact that our friends had posted us.

We must have fun too, nicht? Franke was a good sort. Not much to look at, a bit plump round the hips, but she had long glossy brown hair that fell in waves around her face. Tonight, we go out, you and me. Well, I was tired of feeling like the beachside equivalent of a wallflower. I dressed for my night out with Franke in a slinky blue dress with spaghetti straps that showed off my legs, my best feature, and brought out the blue in my eyes.

Where are we going, then? I asked as we traipsed down to the hotel entrance, trailing clouds of perfume behind us. We go to have dinner, then we go to a club I know. She grinned in a wicked way I didn't quite trust.

After dinner we strolled to the club, which was only a five minute walk away from the hotel. As we approached the entrance I could hear reggae music blasting out. The crowd lining up to get in was mostly tourists, faces all pink and shiny. As we waited in line the music was so loud I could almost feel the bass from the sound system vibrating the air. Franke started dancing on the spot, swaying and moving her hips to a Bob Marley song.

You ladies need an escort for the evening? It was the guy who'd tried to pick me up at the beach bar. He bowed a little with his hand on his heart, kind of sweet, I thought. Franke gave him a quick once over, told him no thanks, we'd got friends inside. He stepped back, still smiling, told us if we changed our minds, he'd still be there.

Just then the queue moved forward and we were swept into a dimly-lit open space about the size of a football pitch. At one end was a bar crowded with bodies and at the other, a mountain of speakers. The ground in between was thick with people dancing. I liked being in the open-air on a warm night, with a sea breeze blowing. Looking up I could see big, bright clusters of stars, like there was a city up there in the sky and we were down here, looking up at its lights. I felt something hovering in the air, something heady and kind of magical, but maybe I was reacting to the clouds of marijuana.

Neither Franke nor I wanted to take on the crowd at the bar, so we didn't bother with drinks. We found a spot and started dancing. The DJ played a lot of oldies I used to dance to as a kid. I gazed around, checking out the talent. The music was good and I was enjoying myself, so I didn't notice what Franke was up to. I turned round to look for her and there she was, wrapped around this guy, smooching as though this was her last chance in life. The guy's face was buried in her neck, so all I could see was the slim shape of his body and his dreadlocks. I felt like a fool, I felt mad as hell but I would have looked stupid just walking out alone. So I held my spot and kept my feet moving, but I felt like the loneliest idiot in the world.

★

Now take a night like tonight. I'm looking cool in my best white pants, my black silk shirt. Feeling cool too. I smoke a spliff on the road, I have another one in my back pocket. The music is *nice,* my kind of oldies. And the place *ram* full of girls. Aha. See that one in the blue frock? She was too good to talk to me the other day. Her friend get a hook up; look at her now she feeling lonely! Yes, my girl, I'm coming.

★

I have to admit I was glad when I noticed him standing by the bar. Yeah, he was quite good looking: no dress sense though. White trousers and black shirt! But his skin glowed like polished wood, and when he caught my eye and smiled, he looked quite gorgeous. Franke and her partner were grinding a hole in the ground to a Gregory Isaacs' song, but though I wanted to dance with this guy, I wanted him to keep a decent distance.

My name is B, he said, coming up close. Short for Baltimore. What's yours?

Suzy, I said and stepped back. He took the hint, and we danced for a bit, just enjoying the music.

I see your friend find herself a soldier, he said. What about you? He moved up close and took hold of my arm. Oh! What the hell. I didn't move away, and he moved even closer and whispered in my ear: You're really sweet, you know. I said nothing. Yeah. Sweet as an Easter lily.

I didn't know what an Easter lily was, but I liked the sound of it. I like the way he breathed the words softly in my ear.

You are a flower, he whispered, his arms tight around me all of a sudden, and I am a B. Together we could make honey. I surprised myself: I giggled. I put my arms round his neck and threw my head back and laughed at him. He smiled back, showing those gorgeous teeth.

You're sweet, I said.

He smiled again and gently pulled my head onto his shoulder.

ELEPHANT DREAMS

Last night I dreamed of flying again and I woke up feeling restless. I got out of bed, fixed some coffee and sat by the kitchen window gazing at the sky. The morning was fine for the time of year: March, midway between winter and spring. Sunlight glowed like a slow fire in my kitchen, yet a chill wind was teasing the buds on the plane trees outside. The wind and the trees spoke to me, quiet murmurs of movement, murmurs that made me feel like travelling.

The flying dream was not new, neither was the urge for change. These past few months the longing would take hold of me suddenly, out of nowhere, the way other people might crave something comforting: a favourite food, a toy from childhood, their mother perhaps. You could read escapism into this, or a poor adjustment to the rhythms of normal existence, but you would be wrong. I enjoy my life most of the time. I enjoy my work: teaching history in a large comprehensive school. I can even take pleasure in routine – in the daily order of eating, working, eating, resting, eating, sleeping – as I would in a long, slow dance. But I have these dreams and these restless feelings and they unsettle me.

An old boyfriend from Mali once told me about an extraordinary people who roam his country, the Faanu. Their whole existence is designed for movement. They own no land, no property, nothing they cannot carry with them on their journeys. To the Faanu stability is hell, heaven is a fresh horizon, a new landscape, unbroken ground on which to rest for a season or two. You have Faanu blood in you, my friend used to say.

I didn't always dream of flying. When I was a child I rode elephants in my dreams. Night after night I rode through a forest, on an elephant's back. I wore robes of scarlet and gold, and carried a sabre which I used to cut a trail through the overhanging tangle of leaves, branches and aerial roots. The cries of birds and the screeches and calls of wild beasts filled the air with noise. A tiger appeared from behind a tree, froze, then retreated. A macaw swooped beside me, flashing its sapphire feathers and cackling in my ear. The elephant strode on and I rode its back as if on a small boat on a tireless wave, rising and then falling.

My childhood home was a terraced house in the heart of North London's Caribbean community. My parents, Don and Louise Samson, and myself, Jewel, occupied the top two floors. The self-contained flat on the lower floor was rented, first to a couple from Barbados, next, to two young Antiguan nurses, and shortly after my seventh birthday, to the Kapoors, who had recently migrated from India.

As a child, I didn't understand why my mother disliked the Kapoors. She, who loved to eat chicken curry, complained about their cooking smells. She complained that the soft cloud of incense which hovered around their front door, which I would inhale in greedy breaths each time I passed, made her nose itch. And the sight of Mrs Kapoor's saris draped on washing lines across the back garden, fluttering in the wind like brilliant silken flags, was offensive enough to bring on an attack of nerves.

I did not heed my mother's antipathy. In the summer holidays I played in the back garden with Ismet, the Kapoors' young son. Our garden was long, with rose borders, a lawn and two apple trees at the bottom. Ismet and I were close in age and rampant with energy. We climbed the apple trees, racing to see who could reach the top first, and who could slither to the ground fastest. We played tag, chasing each other around the lawn till we were breathless and ready to collapse.

When young apples fell from the trees we gathered them for Mrs Kapoor to make chutney. I hovered in her kitchen, curious and greedy, while she chopped up onions and garlic, and tossed them into a great iron pan with the apples and a mix of spices. The fruity scent of chutney simmering filled the kitchen and spread through the entire house.

You like to taste, no? Mrs Kapoor said when the chutney was done.

Yes, yes, I want to taste, I said.

I give you some, she said, for your family.

For my family? I was doubtful, suspecting that my mother would fling any offering from Mrs Kapoor straight into the dustbin. Yet I wanted to taste that chutney so badly I hid the jar in my bedroom, at the bottom of my wardrobe. At night when I was alone, I retrieved the jar and dug into it with my fingers. I would fill my mouth with apple and spice and pepper and oil, savouring the succulent mixture of flavours on my tongue.

The Kapoors moved away before I turned eight, but the elephant dream, which started soon after they moved in, continued for years, night after night, repeating and repeating and repeating.

★

At twenty-four, I was tall and slender, with a head full of baby braids. Very little of importance had happened in my life until then. I had spent three years at a northern university where I was cold most of the time, and lonely. I was involved in a half-baked affair with an accountant from Trinidad which should have died from neglect, but which kept limping along. I worked as a supply teacher, moving from school to school, a new placement every two or three weeks, each move a challenge to my endurance. At twenty-four, I wondered was this all there was?

Arjun said I used to walk past him on the high street, always in a hurry. He wanted to stop me, to talk to me, he said, but I would pass by without seeing him, a faraway look in my eyes. Once he saw me with Daryl, the accountant, walking together, but not touching, not holding hands. He could tell we were lovers. He could tell we were not in love.

I met Arjun DasGupta at the Star of India, a small restaurant not far from my flat. It was Saturday lunchtime and the restaurant was crowded.

Do you mind if I sit here? he said. There's nowhere else.

Oh, no, please do, I said, responding to his warm smile and rich, accented voice.

You must live around here, he said, sitting down. I've seen you on the high street quite often…

I live just around the corner. I closed the book I was reading and took in his tightly curling black hair, his sparkling teeth, his brown eyes that reflected light.

I live three blocks down the road, and I come here almost every day – the paneer is *very* good!

It is. It's what I usually have, but today, I felt like channa.

Are you from Africa? He glanced at my head which was wrapped in African fabric.

Several generations ago. My parents are from Jamaica. And you?

I'm from India. Calcutta.

Calcutta!

I'm here doing research, at Imperial College.

Oh yes? On what?

On the behaviour of light particles. Particles of light, that is.

Over channa battura and sag paneer, he explained the basic principles of particle theory: how light particles respond to atmospheric conditions; how some move in waves and others in a straight line; how, when viewed through a microscope, they respond to a spectator's gaze, changing behaviour accordingly. Enthusiasm for his subject lit up his face and kept his hands in motion, like the waves he described. He made science sound magical.

Does that mean nothing real in itself? I asked.

Oh no. It means a thing is what you think it is. It's all in the mind.

Everything? Even non-material things?

Everything, he said.

I had a feeling he was laughing at me, so I changed the subject. I asked him about Calcutta: was it as poor and awful a place as it was said to be? His response surprised me. He spoke about Calcutta's vitality, its cultural richness, and the resourcefulness of its people. His eyes glowed and his speech grew rapid, emphatic. Sometimes he tripped on his tongue in his eagerness and it struck me that he was lonely. Only lonely people talk so passionately to strangers.

Enough about me, he said eventually. Tell me about you.

I talked about the trials of supply teaching, and about my dancing, the only reliable joy in my life. He asked about my family, and I told him my parents' story, how they came to London from Jamaica when I was a child.

So, you are a Black Briton!

I prefer Afro-European. Or better still, Diaspora African.

They are only terms, he said, shrugging.

They're more than that! Those terms define who I am. It's different for you. You're Indian, plain and simple.

Being Indian is neither of those things, he said. And the rest of your life? Will it be here, in England?

That was a question I wished I could answer, for myself as well as for him. But who at twenty-four knows what even the next month will bring?

Who knows? I said. I hope not, though. I'd like to travel in Africa... Ghana, Senegal, Nigeria... I want to set foot at least once on the land of my ancestors. And I would love to visit India!

You would? His eyes widened, alight with surprise.

Oh yes. For a long time I used to dream of India... or what I thought was India! Forests, elephants, tigers...

How curious. He gazed at me quizzically. And do you follow your dreams?

I'd like to. The place in my dreams always felt... it's hard to explain... felt familiar... Isn't that odd?

I used to think I had African blood, he said, teeth gleaming in a wide smile. Don't laugh: just look at the colour of my skin! Look at the kink in my hair!

I laughed, we both laughed. He reached across the table and touched my hand.

Once I had met Arjun, leaving Daryl, the Trinidadian

was easy. We parted like a loose connection broken by the mildest of tremors. Arjun flowed easily into my life. We met virtually every day after our first encounter at the restaurant. He would telephone with offers of food, which I, lazy after a day at school, or tired after a dance class, would accept. He would be on my doorstep within minutes with a meal packed up in tupperware. Sometimes he took me across London into the far corners of Whitechapel, an area previously unknown to me, in search of authentic Bengali cooking. He took me to art house cinemas, to festivals of Indian films, to South Bank concerts of Indian music, to restaurants and to pubs with acquaintances and colleagues from India. I was not used to so much activity, so much talk. My intellect, which had gone into retirement after college, came vigorously back to life.

Did I wonder what future there was for us? I don't think I did, at least not in our early months together. But in retrospect, I can see that he did: from the beginning our steps forward were instigated by him.

One morning we lay languidly in my bed, our limbs entwined.

You see, he had said, holding his arm against mine, I am as black as you.

You're Indian black. That's different.

What difference? There's none.

I used to think there was, I said, teasing him. I used to think Indian men had small penises and didn't know how to make love.

Some Indian men do have small penises, but didn't you know the population of India doubles itself with each generation? Why is that, do you think?

Poverty. Ignorance. Inadequate birth control...

We wrote the *Kama Sutra* centuries ago. That should

tell you something. What did Africans write?

Hieroglyphics, I said. And maps of the cosmos. On the walls of pyramids.

Not the same time-frame, he said, his arms encircling me, pulling me closer to kiss me. I love being with you. We're so different, yet good together. We should live together, don't you think?

It's too soon. It's only been three months, one week, and two days…

We are almost living together now.

My place is too small, and yours is tiny.

Then we find somewhere else! What is this reluctance?

It's not reluctance, I said. Living together is a big, big, step. I pulled away from his arms. Besides, what will I do when you go back home to Calcutta?

You'll come with me, of course. Is there anything you'd rather do?

What could I say to that? Before Arjun, I had nothing but doubts about my future. Now, I let myself be persuaded by his confidence in us as a couple, which was far, far stronger than my confidence in myself.

The following Saturday my best friend Celia and I went shopping in Covent Garden, one of our favourite pastimes. As we walked through the Piazza, I draped my arm around her shoulders, and leaned on her sturdy frame like a woman weary from love. I asked her advice about living with Arjun.

Don't be daft! She shook her head emphatically and her Afro trembled like a black, ominous cloud. He's leaving in a few months. Why set yourself up for heartache?

You're right, I sighed. And there's my Mum… she'd go crazy!

I know you really care for him, and everything, but…
He says I should go home with him.
To Calcutta? Is he insane?
I took her arm as we headed out of the Piazza towards the tube. She moved so purposefully, each step planted firmly on the ground. I felt reassured just keeping pace with her.
I'd consider going if I thought he *really* meant it.
Celia stopped in her tracks, rounding on me.
You would *what*? You'd leave your family, your friends, your job…?
They're important, but they're not everything, you know!
No, I don't know, she said. I don't know at all.
I don't know what I'd do without him.

★

It was early spring when Arjun moved in with me. Daffodils were everywhere, trumpeting hope and happiness from every flower bed in my neighbourhood. He came with crates of books and shelves which covered two walls in the living room. He took charge of the kitchen with no opposition from me, building extra shelves to accommodate his extensive collection of pots, pans and spices. Arjun loved to cook almost as much as he loved to talk. He seduced me from my temperate diet with luscious creamy curries, fragrant pillaus, and *subjis* spiked with chillies, ginger and too much garlic. He had learned to cook from his grandmother. She had spent her adult life rearing children and cooking delicious meals for her husband and family. After just a few weeks of his cooking my breasts grew heavy, my legs too, and my hips filled out voluptuously. This was hard on my clothes, which strained at the seams, but it was very good for my dancing.

We knew he would have to return home at some point after the summer, but we avoided talking about it. It was too big and sad an issue for me to anticipate. Faintheartedly, I hoped that when the day arrived he would leave without pain or participation from me. Then, as summer approached, I noticed him changing. He spent longer hours at the library and came home twitchy and irritable. He was often too tired to make love, but even worse, he lost interest in cooking.

One morning he jumped up in bed, declaring: Jewel, I have to go home soon. I have to go back and look for a job.

When are you going? I mumbled, in a sudden panic, thinking the beginning of the end had arrived.

The first week in July. Come with me! Come see if you can live in India.

Arjun, it's not that simple! Part of me really wants to but… well… what will I do there? Will I fit in? Will your parents accept me?

What do you mean? Of course they'll like you!

So why have you been so strange lately, hmmm? I think you've been worrying about going home with a black girl on your arm!

You don't understand. My parents are civilized. They both went to Cambridge…

So…? His logic escaped me sometimes.

They made friends from Africa, the West Indies, from all over the world. Besides, I've written them and told them about you. I'm worried, as you say, more about whether you will come, whether you will like it there. Life is so different in India…

I know that.

You don't. Not really. You have never seen poverty. You say you want to see India but I suspect that is just a fantasy.

Arjun, I know that poverty exists…

And my family… we live very different to this. He made a sweep of his arm.

And you think I won't be able to adjust?

Come for a few weeks and then make up your mind. You won't know otherwise.

He sat on the bed, tugging my hand like a pleading child to make me agree. Which I did. I agreed to fly out to Calcutta for a month as soon as school was over. And I surrendered completely to anticipation of that journey, so that when the time came for him to leave, the promise of that month together helped us cope with his departure. As we packed his belongings for shipping, we pretended we were merely shifting location, that we were simply making changes in preparation for a future together in Calcutta.

Since meeting Arjun I had read, seen and heard so much about India that I departed for Calcutta believing I knew what to expect. Within minutes of arriving I realised nothing could have prepared me for that teeming, pulsating, decaying sprawl.

The first sight of the city overwhelms me. Imagine: more people than you could ever imagine inhabiting one urban space. Imagine Chowringee, the city's most elegant street, choked with traffic from dawn to midnight, with ancient cars, hand-pulled rickshaws, cycle rickshaws, scooter rickshaws, buffalo carts, smoke-belching trucks, buses with passengers riding on top, on the sides, hanging from the back, perched on the front bumper and even clinging to the bonnet. Pedestrians jaywalking, serene in the conviction that their lives are sacred and protected. Droves of cattle, their lives also sacred, meandering amidst the traffic, garlands of marigolds around their necks, placid as if they were grazing in fields of daisies. Imagine shanties of cardboard erected against every available stretch of wall, the permanent homes of people who work and cook and bathe on the street, and hang marigold garlands around the necks of cows on holy days. Imagine those shanties and the state of the people who live in them during the summer's monsoon rains.

Arjun collects me from the airport in his family's decrepit Morris. I feel a burst of happiness when I see him, smiling and familiar in these strange surroundings. I hug and kiss him throughout the ride to his parents' house. His parents, sister, uncle and grandmother are waiting for us at the door of their sprawling bungalow, which is covered in vibrant red and pink bougainvillea. I climb out of the car and ascend the steps, feeling crumpled and grimy from travel, and all too aware of eyes watching me.

Jewel, meet my parents! Arjun stands close, one arm across my shoulder. And my grandmother, my Uncle Partha and my sister Shireen.

Welcome, my child! Arjun's mother is tiny, with a chignon almost as large as her head. She embraces me, barely touching both my cheeks with hers. Arjun's father smiles charmingly, saying, Ah yes! A jewel indeed! He is thin and wiry, and his eyes crease at the corners. His shock of greying hair curls tightly, like Arjun's.

I have been *so* looking forward to meeting you, says Shireen, whose warm voice is low and rich. She is beautiful, with hair cascading to her waist and sparkling eyes. I shake hands with Uncle Partha who bows slightly and withdraws into the house. Grandmother doesn't shake hands. Her lips remain pursed, a thin line in a round face. When I say hello, she looks me up and down, but says nothing. Her scrutiny makes me wish I could disappear, or fade out of sight.

Come, child, let me show you to your room so you can freshen up. Are you hungry? Would you like tea? Yes? Shireen, ask Ousman to prepare tea, and Arjun, bring along Jewel's luggage, please. Mrs DasGupta's voice is brisk, crisp. She leads me down a shadowy hallway to a room at the far end of the house chattering about the rains, the heat, the mosquitoes.

The mosquitoes are dreadful right now, she is saying, I hope you are taking your anti-malaria pills? I examine the wood-panelled walls, the high shine of the worn tiles on the floor. The musty air, laced with traces of sandal-wood, takes me back in time, calling to mind Mrs Kapoor whom I haven't thought of in years. I recall the smell of incense and chutney and whispering silk saris – an oddly jarring recollection since there is really little similarity between the soft woman I knew as a child and the crisp, efficient woman beside me.

Here you are, she says, opening the door of a room twice the size of my bedroom in London. The bathroom is just there. She indicates a half open door leading off the bedroom. Please, rest as long as you like. Join us when you are ready. If there's anything you need, just ask Ousman, the bearer, when he brings your tea. She smiles, nods and withdraws.

Minutes later Ousman taps on the door, bearing a tray with tea things and biscuits. He is dressed in blue twill, and his face is mournful and droopy, rather like a camel. Arjun follows behind him, carrying my luggage. He has changed into a white *kurta pyjama*. Against the bright cotton his skin looks darker than it did in London. He is more alluring than ever.

I didn't think we'd be in separate rooms... I say, wrapping my arms around him.

My mother is very traditional, he says, but don't worry, my room is just across the hall.

You didn't tell me your family is rich... This house is palatial! I am most impressed by the bed, a huge mahogany four poster draped with mosquito nets.

I told you they are university professors, he shrugs. Are you tired? Do you want to take a nap? There will be plenty of time to meet the family properly later on.

We kiss and he leaves me to sleep. I am hot, tired and disoriented. I climb into the enormous bed and adjust the mosquito net around it. I fall asleep in a second and I dream I am deep in my familiar forest riding pillion on an elephant, with Arjun behind me, holding me safely in his arms.

Arjun's mother is very attentive to my needs. Food, laundry, entertainment: she takes care of everything. In the morning over breakfast she checks our plans for the day, suggesting this place to visit, that place to go for good shopping. She moves like a bird, darting here and there, quick and sharp. She is considerate but not warm. I sense her watching me, but when I catch her eye, she smiles, a quick, momentary movement of the lips.

Arjun shows me the sights of Calcutta, which are mainly Victorian monuments, but also places to shop and eat. I am charmed by Cottage Industries, a craft emporium on Chowringee decorated in the style of a rajah's palace. A bevy of demure young women in crisp cotton saris watch while I pore over silver jewellery that costs next to nothing by London standards, and drool over hand-embroidered bedlinen that costs little more than Woolworth's polyester sheets. Arjun buys me a small soapstone carving of an elephant dancing on hind legs, trunk waving in the air. He waits patiently while I buy linen for my mother, earrings for Celia, a bangle for myself. The women's curiosity is so insistent, I sigh with relief as we walk out of the store.

Is that normal, I ask as we make our way to the car. Staring like that: is it normal here?

Arjun shrugs. They have never seen an Afro-European before.

He takes me to New Market, where everyone in the city who can afford to do so shops for flowers, fruit, vegetables, and everything imaginable for the home. We stroll in the flower market, amid iron buckets full of blazing marigolds, blushing peonies, huge chrysanthemums and purple Michaelmas daisies. Arjun buys a garland of tuberoses and hangs it around my neck. Their heady scent perfumes my way through the musty market.

We stop at a stall decked with pyramids of mangoes. Arjun looks carefully before buying, touching and smelling the fruit.

The best Alphonsos, *sahib,* the very best! The vendor speaks fluent English and is eager to make conversation.

Madam, where do you come from? He bows politely, but his eyes dart from Arjun's face to mine. Arjun is engrossed in the mangos.

Take a guess.

The vendor ponders a moment.

America.

No, guess again.

He examines my clothes, my shoes, my hair and shrugs.

I'm from England. I force a polite smile.

Ohhh? You do not look like an English lady! He frowns and scratches his head.

You've challenged his understanding of the world, Arjun says as we walk away from the stall.

Arjun's parents are both professors at Calcutta University, he of physics, she of anaesthesiology. I hardly see them during the daytime, nor Grandmother, nor Uncle Partha. They keep to their rooms, working, reading, or in Grandmother's case, cooking. I read a lot and sleep a lot, and in the evenings I play cards with Arjun and Shireen, who are teaching me the game of bridge.

The monsoon season is under way. Rain pours down in torrents for days and there is flooding everywhere in the city. Water swirls around the DasGuptas' yard with branches and garbage and dead rats floating in it. The morning after the rain breaks Arjun rolls up his pants and wades out to run errands for his parents. I stay indoors, avoiding all contact with the polluted water, but the air inside the house is so thick, almost vaporous, it is hard to breathe deeply. I am housebound for six damp, miserable days during which time everything capable of absorption takes on a cold, clammy quality: the sheets on my bed, my clothes in the closet, the pages of the book I am reading.

The day after the rains cease, Shireen persuades me to go out with her in the Morris, which Arjun obligingly brings right up against the front steps so we can avoid stepping in water. Shireen takes me to a *jyotishi* to have my chart read. The *jyotishi* lives in Ballygunge, not far from the DasGupta's home. To get there, we splash through narrow roads lined with the skeletal remains of lean-to dwellings stripped of their cardboard walls by the rain.

How do these people manage? Where do they go when their shelter and belongings get washed away?

They start again, says Shireen. They rebuild, they retrieve what they can from the flood and start afresh. Every year after the monsoon, it's the same. Her matter-of-fact tone, the absence of admiration or regret, repels me. I stare at her youthful profile and wonder: what makes a young person so tolerant of poverty and devastation? Her profile offers no clues.

Shireen parks close to the entrance to the *jyotishi's* house, but we must wade through murky water to reach his door. A young woman in a yellow cotton sari shows us into a tiny room smoky with incense. An altar decked with dishes of food rests against a wall, presided over by a statue of an elephant seated human-style, back legs folded, front legs extended like arms, garlands of bright orange marigolds draped around its neck. The statue is about four feet tall and carved out of grey marble.

That is Ganesh, Shireen whispers, our god of luck and prosperity.

We sit on cushions on the floor awaiting the astrologer. Shireen's eyelashes flutter; there is colour in her cheeks. She is the picture of girlish anticipation, as though her future was to be told rather than mine. I do not share her excitement. I am not sure I want to know what the future has in store just yet.

The astrologer enters the room carrying a large, thick book under his arm. His belly is enormous, his hair thin and oily. He wears a crisp muslin *dhoti* and a raw silk *kurta*. He sits facing us on the floor, cross-legged on a cushion, the book beside him. The spine of the book is broken, the cloth cover faded and marked by frequent use. The *jyotishi* bows in greeting, asks my time and place of birth, and then consults the book. Shireen and I wait in silence while he calculates my chart.

Do you have any particular concerns, madam? The lining of his mouth is stained red from chewing *beetel* nut; his gums look as if they are bleeding.

I hesitate, but Shireen is quick to respond.

When will she marry? Will she have many children?

He nods, re-examines the chart, then jots a few notes on a piece of paper.

I see here that she is dedicated to learning, he says to Shireen. She will spend her life among scholars.

Well, I am a schoolteacher... I interrupt him abruptly, aware that I am being rude, but I'm offended that he addressed his remarks to Shireen.

You have a long journey ahead of you. He speaks to me directly this time, his voice a nasal drone.

Back to London, perhaps?

Shireen nudges my side and glares.

Many journeys, very many. Yes! You are a traveller!

But will she marry soon? The sharp tone of Shireen's voice betrays her true concern.

I do not see it here, he says. But she will marry, and she will have children. That is all I can tell you now.

Suddenly, I want to know what the elephant god Ganesh intends for me. I want to ask about my luck, about my future prosperity, but before I can speak my question, the *jyotishi* rises and walks out of the room, leaving Shireen and I to follow suit.

After the floods subside, Arjun's parents throw a small party, inviting relatives mainly, but also a few university people and some of Arjun's old friends. Shortly before the guests are due to arrive, Shireen enters the living room wearing a sari of turquoise silk shot with a deep green thread. The fabric shimmers when she moves, like a tropical sea under moonlight. I feel dowdy and inappropriate in a light blue cotton shift, like a stray weed pushing up its head beside a hot-house flower.

I should lend you a sari! Shireen says. She senses my discomfort, and is being kind, but her offer makes me feel even more self conscious, even more out of place.

It would suit you, she says. In a sari, you would look Indian, almost. It is only... She gestures towards my head of coiling braids.

It is too late to change clothes now, I say, shaking my head so my braids lift and move. But thanks. Some other time, maybe.

She leaves the room and returns moments later with a scarf draped over an arm.

I was planning to give you this as a gift when... later on. She offers me the scarf, a length of peacock-coloured gossamer embroidered around the edges in gold.

It will look nice with your dress, I think. Please, will you wear it this evening?

I drape the scarf over my shoulders. Even without a mirror I can tell it transforms my dress from everyday to elegant. It transforms my appearance, though not the way I feel. But I hug Shireen to show my thanks and we sit together to await the arrival of guests.

Dinner is served buffet style, on silver platters laid out on a carved mahogany table in the dining room. Grandmother stands to one side of the table, hands clasped to her chest, nodding in approval as the guests pile food onto their plates. Grandmother has excelled herself: the guests, myself included, return for second and third helpings. As I leave the table for the third time, I compliment Grandmother on her cooking. She inclines her head in a sideways nod and averts her gaze, as though denying my presence, my words. I turn my back on her, the taste of her food turning bitter in my mouth.

After dinner, we sit out on the long verandah in rickety wicker chairs, clustered in groups. Some play Scrabble, some play bridge, others chatter noisily, gossiping or discussing the news of the day. Ousman drifts among the guests fetching glasses of beer or soda or *nimbu pani*. I feel unsettled by the strangeness of it all: the sound of Bengali being spoken around me, the lavish dinner, the heat, the humidity, the smell of decay in the air.

Arjun introduces me to his cousin Reetinder, who has a paunch, and a loud, boisterous manner, like an English public school boy. He works for an international bank and talks intensely about the price of shares on the Calcutta stock exchange. He is so completely unlike Arjun I find it hard to believe they are related. He and I are on the edge of a larger group: we fall into conversation.

Arjun tells me you are from the West Indies.

My parents come from Jamaica, I explain.

Ha! So you are a displaced person!

I – I don't see myself that way. His directness startles me into stuttering.

All immigrants are displaced persons.

That is rubbish, Reeti, and you know it! Arjun must have been eavesdropping. He moves closer to me and puts an arm around my shoulders.

So, how do you like Calcutta? Reetinder asks, changing tack.

It's rather different from London…

Oh yes, very different! He laughs, though I don't see the joke.

You need special skills to survive this mess, he adds, not to mention cast-iron lungs and intestines, what with all the pollution and the floods.

Reeti is always complaining about our city, Arjun explains. I think he would prefer not to be here.

Be honest, Arjun! Does anyone really want to be here? Reeti asks. I think that if we could all get visas to England or the USA, everyone here would leave.

You're wrong, says Arjun. Many of us stay because we belong here; because this is home.

Yes! shouts Reeti, triumphant. My point exactly. Anything is better than being displaced.

Let us stop here, Reeti, or we'll end up quarrelling! Arjun pulls me to my feet. Jewel, come and meet my aunt Mira.

Later that night Arjun creeps into my room. We lie in bed, discussing the evening's events in whispers.

I don't know what has happened to Reeti, says Arjun. Banking – it has made him so conservative!

I think he's right about immigrants and displacement, I say. I just didn't want to admit it to him at the time. And you agree with him, sort of, don't you? You think people should stay where they belong.

No, no! How can you say that?

It's probably true, I say matter-of-factly. Away from London, I definitely feel out of place.

And here? How do you feel here?

Can't you tell? Can't you see? Wherever I go, people stare at me like I'm some kind of freak!

I am lying on my back, one hand behind my head, the other worrying a braid. I recall my dream of safe passage through the jungle and the feeling of security, cradled by Arjun, high on the elephant's back. I am thinking how far from safe I feel in Arjun's home, with his grandmother's hostility and his mother's briskness. I am thinking of dreams and how misleading they can be and the thought brings on a gush of tears.

I don't understand how people cope here, I say, making an effort to keep my voice steady. The poverty, the garbage everywhere; the flooding, the chaos. How do they stay sane?

That is not what they look at, says Arjun. That is not what they see. He moves closer and buries his face in the hollow of my shoulder. I breathe deep, preparing to speak the words I know will wound us both.

I don't think I could live here, Arjun. I circle him with my arms and rest my cheek against his head.

This is the worst possible time to be here. His words are muffled, buried against my skin. Calcutta is at its worst in the monsoon.

You know I'm not talking about the weather.

His head on my shoulder is still and heavy. I hear his breath, I feel the soft beat of his heart against my side. He says nothing.

I returned to London and wept hot torrents of gritty tears for an entire week. When the tears ceased I felt listless, drained and numb inside, as though a vital organ had been removed. I slept through most of the remaining days of the summer recess, unable to throw off disappointment, unwilling to face the blank screen my life had become without Arjun.

Three weeks after my return, I received a letter from him, a single sheet of brittle airmail paper covered with his minute, fastidious script. Anger throbbed in the spaces between the neatly formed words. Hurt too, but I felt his anger like a blade digging at my heart.

I have applied for the position of research assistant
at the Centre for Scientific Research in Ranchi, which
is in Bihar, the state just north of Bengal. You would

like Ranchi, I think. It is quiet and very clean, but I will not ask you to consider joining me there. I see now that I was your opportunity for adventure, for exotic experience. I know now that you only loved me because of your elephant dream.

I put the letter away in a bureau drawer. I was unable to reply. I lacked the strength to provide the reassurance the letter cried out for, or the energy to convince myself that Arjun was wrong.

When the new school year began, with a daunting new set of rowdy students, I was already exhausted. I moved sluggishly from day to day, like a six-cylinder car running with three cylinders down. Every night I fell into a sleep that was like falling into a dark pit, without even the comfort of dreams. Every morning I woke up with a sinking heart, thinking: So. This is all there is.

My mother called me every evening and fussed down the phone. She was convinced I had picked up something in India.

Go to the doctor, she said, get a check up. He'll give you something to make you feel better.

My mother thought doctors could fix everything.

You need medicine.

I need time.

Listen to me, she said. You will need less time if you get medication.

My mother's logic overwhelmed me. I agreed to see a doctor, but the next day I changed my mind. My bones told me that if a cure for my malaise existed, it would be neither medical nor chemical. I needed to talk to someone, but my conversations with Celia didn't help much. I found it hard to discuss my feelings about Arjun with her. She made sympathetic noises, but she thought I'd brought heartache on myself. I was tempted to seek help from a phone-in counsellor. But instead, in a moment of impulse, I dialled a number I'd seen advertised in a magazine and made an appointment for a consultation with a spiritual reader.

The consulting room was a small storefront at the back of Brixton market, out of the way of the crowds of shoppers. As I stepped through the door a woman dressed entirely in white appeared from behind a curtain at the back. She was middle-aged, with skin that shone like a roasted coffee bean. She stared into my face without smiling, then beckoned me to follow her behind the curtain.

Miss Samson? Ah, yes. Here is where I do all the work. Her voice was clear, her accent French. Was she Haitian? West African?

The small room smelled of incense and was lit by candles, their light flickering and dim. There were two chairs at a table spread with glasses of water, more candles, shells, pieces of rock. She motioned to me to sit facing her.

Jewel Elizabeth Samson. She wrote my name on a piece of paper. How can I help you? Her gaze on my face was intent, as if she was already reading something there.

I hesitated, not knowing what to say.

You need guidance, perhaps? Her face softened.

Yes. I do. I replied. And… direction.

She explained the proceedings and the cost. Then she took a handful of shells and shook them, chanting in an unfamiliar language. She threw the shells on the table, scrutinised them with narrowed eyes, then wrote on the sheet of paper. She repeated this action three more times. Then she began to speak.

A woman migrates from the east to the west.

Oh, I said, I've recently come back from a holiday in India.

This could be someone else; it might not be you, she said. Perhaps someone in your past. A relative, an ancestor, perhaps?

I don't have any Indian ancestors. I was already impatient and irritated by the hocus pocus, the chanting and the shells. My family are from the West Indies; our ancestors came from Africa.

She smiled, a faint, knowing smile.

Often we do not know what is in our past.

I shrugged, regretting the impulse that had brought me.

You are confused, she said gently. You do not know what you really want. You think you want this, you think you want that, but you do not know for certain.

Well, yes… I suppose that is true… I shrugged again.

She read from the sheet of paper.

The egret has eaten flying fish.

I spread my hands to register incomprehension.

The egret is a bird and birds must fly. The fish it eats makes it restless.

A chill shot up my spine, as if my back was suddenly naked, exposed and cold.

You have lost your home and you are travelling, she said. All the same, like the egret, you must build a nest.

Another chill, a sudden flash, like the shock of a sluice of iced water. Impatience and irritation vanished. My head cleared and I understood what she was telling me: I was the egret.

Perhaps I should stop…? She paused, watching my face.

No, please carry on. I'm fine, really, I said, and forced

94

a smile. I probably need to hear this… even if I don't understand fully.

She read once more from the paper.

Beyond the mountains are more mountains.

I raised my hands in surrender.

Examine your expectations, she said. Life is difficult in every place, in every land. There are mountains everywhere. Only your perception of things makes a difference between what you find in one place or another.

Calcutta came to mind and I open my mouth to argue. No shift of consciousness could erase poverty and squalor. Then I thought of Arjun and particle theory. I heard his voice explaining how light particles respond to the observer's gaze. I remembered Shireen's serene adjustment to the destruction wrought by the flood, and I kept quiet.

The woman folded the paper and handed it to me.

Is that all? I was ready to hear more. I *needed* to hear more.

She nodded. Go and make peace with your life.

That night, for the first time in weeks, I slept deeply, and I dreamed. In that dream I was a bird, and I was flying.

COMING HOME

When the doorbell rang, Abena was flopped on the only chair not laden with boxes. Her head thrown back, dreadlocks spilling over the back of the chair, she drew deep, long breaths on the butt of a spliff. Stacks of boxes jostled for space with furniture swathed in plastic – items she had carefully wrapped up in her old apartment in Albany. Only the chair on which she sat and a life-size papier-mâché sculpture of a banana tree in full leaf were free of wrapping.

Whaddya do with all of this stuff? One of the movers had asked, a stocky guy with thinning hair, quizzing the banana tree. *Enough stuff here to fill a house. And you alone? Tell me, whaddya do with it all?* He rubbed his balding head and left Abena questioning her habit of buying and holding onto thrift-store finds she really didn't need. But just looking at the banana tree made her feel a little spark of warmth. It reminded her of home and that made it worth keeping, even if its colourful foliage and fruit were at odds with the beige of its new surroundings.

Earlier, she had unpacked tea things and brewed a cup of mint tea. Mint tea and marijuana: taken together, the ultimate comfort. The spliff exhausted, she discarded the butt and cradled the mug of tea in both hands. She surveyed the beige walls and high ceilings. The room opened onto a kitchen through an arch on one side and onto the hallway through an arch on the other. The apartment was big enough to accommodate two people with a lot of belongings, or even a couple with a child. Its bareness made Abena anxious to cover the walls with pictures, to fill the kitchen cupboards with her assortment of blue-and-white china dishes and plates, to fill its closets with her clothes, but the prospect of doing those things made her feel weary. Another new place to make into a home. Even though this time the place was all her own, the lease in her name, she felt no excitement, only the gentle languor that smoking induced. Had she been wise to give up her job in Albany to come back to Brooklyn?

★

Perhaps she was destined not to settle, not to put down roots anywhere. Until she was ten, she had lived in Jamaica with her mother, Lisette, and her half-sister, Keisha, in a poky apartment in Willowdene, just outside Spanish Town and not far from the hospital where her mother worked as a nurse. One morning, a few weeks before Abena's tenth birthday, Lisette was run over by a bus while crossing the road, less than half a mile from her home. The bus driver was drunk, or high, or both. He failed to see Lisette and slammed on his brakes too late. She died on the spot.

It was their neighbour, a stout, kindly woman they called Miss May, who broke the news to the children. Miss May had watched over the young nurse and her girls like a caring relative; she was a widow and retired with plenty of time on her hands. She helped out with simple kindnesses, like keeping the girls after school until Lisette came home and refusing to accept money for doing so. Lisette called her Miss May, but thought of her as family, as did the girls. The morning of Lisette's death, still dizzy with the shock of it, Miss May had tapped on the door of the apartment. Abena's welcoming smile had faded when she saw Miss May's chin quivering.

Miss May took the girls home with her that night and settled them in her guestroom. She had never met Abena's father and she had seen Keisha's father only once, on one of his rare visits. But Keisha's father had seen the report of Lisette's death on television and came knocking on Miss May's door the next evening. He came to take Keisha, but when Miss May asked what to do about Abena, he simply shook his head. *He was sorry 'bout Abena, but she wasn't his child. Don't Lisette have a sister in New York? Maybe Miss May should call her. Strange how far death's hand can reach. But maybe Abena would have better luck if her aunt brought her to America.*

★

Miss May made all the arrangements for Abena's move to her aunt's house in Brooklyn. By the time she was twelve, Abena had given up praying that Keisha would join her there. Keisha's father hadn't left his address with Miss May, and her aunt Pinky showed no interest in finding her other niece. Abena's life in her aunt's house in suburban Brooklyn was quiet, safe, regular. She accepted that her family now was Aunt Pinky, Uncle Teddy and her cousin Claire, but still yearned for the closeness she had felt with her mother and sister. It was hard to believe that the plump flouncy woman with a grating American accent was her mother's sister. Lisette had been reed-thin, with a neat short Afro that capped her clean-scrubbed face; Aunt Pinky was rounded and soft in a bloated, unhealthy way and she wore heavy, orange-tinted make-up that made her look permanently hot. Despite the softness of her body, she was not someone who would hug you and squeeze you till you giggled and begged her to stop. And she never said anything kind or sweet or funny – at least not to Abena. She lavished hugs and kisses on Claire, but then Claire was her own child.

★

Claire. Spoiled, precious Claire, known to her mocking classmates as *Ah de-Claire!* A wry smile curled Abena's lips then faded. Claire had phoned earlier that morning, the first time they had spoken for months. The sound of Claire's voice was so unexpected that had left Abena at a loss for words.

Claire, she blurted eventually. How did you get my number?

From Pops.

Abena regretted the good manners that had compelled her to call her uncle and tell him she had moved back to Brooklyn. Aunt Pinky had died suddenly from a heart attack eighteen months before and Uncle Teddy now lived in the family home with Claire. She had felt safe in thinking that Uncle Teddy would not call; it had not occurred to her that Claire might.

I know it's been a while, Claire continued, but I wanted to welcome you back to Brooklyn… I… I wondered if you needed help with unpacking or anything…

Thanks, but I'm doing fine. I'm almost done. Abena frowned, wondering what lay behind this offer of help. Claire was not given to random acts of kindness.

I just thought… moving can be so stressful. But if you don't need help, maybe we could have a drink sometime soon. You know, a "welcome back to Brooklyn" drink. Uh – how about this evening?

Welcome back to Brooklyn! That was rich! A welcome offered years too late! The words formed on Abena's tongue but she swallowed them.

This evening? What's up? What's so urgent?

Well then, how about coffee, tomorrow afternoon, say at three? At Ossie's on Seventh Avenue?

Oh. Coffee. Sure, if that's what you prefer…

I don't drink much these days. Why don't I come by and pick you up? Then you can show me your apartment.

You want to see the apartment? Oh.

Come on Abena! Of course I want to see your new place!

As Abena searched for a rejoinder, Claire said, Or why don't you make me coffee, and I can help you unpack? Just for a couple of hours. I could be there by one.

All right. If you insist. Abena felt peeved, wishing she'd had the foresight not to answer the phone.

She surveyed the stacked boxes, and the mellow feeling left by the tea and the smoke dispelled. She had told her cousin that she was almost finished unpacking, but she had barely begun. She could use some help, sure, but what configuration of unlucky stars had sent Claire to help her? And why was Claire trying so hard to pretend that there had ever been anything resembling family feeling between them? It was odd, out of character. The unfamiliarity of it made Abena uneasy.

★

When she first came to stay with Aunt Pinky, Abena thought her aunt's house too big for so few people. Her bedroom, though the smallest in the house, felt empty and lonely; she missed snuggling with Keisha in the bed they shared in Willowdene. And the amount of *things*. Abena had to tiptoe through the over-furnished rooms so as not to damage anything. Once, when she was vacuuming her aunt's bedroom, she had accidentally knocked a glass cat from the dresser. The ornament hit the carpet and its head flew clean off. Aunt Pinky chewed her ears off about it for days. *I know you're not used to good things, but don't come break up my things with your yam-hands*, she complained. She held back Abena's pocket money for a month. *Just so you learn the cost of things.*

Claire had shown mild curiosity about Abena when she first arrived. She looked at her young cousin as if surprised, as if she found it strange to be related to such a skinny, morose little thing. Abena's awe at her surroundings amused her; she thought her simple. She could barely speak English; she called the kitchen faucet a *pipe,* she held a cooking-pot by its *hangle* and asked to watch *love flims* on television. Her accent, when it wasn't embarrassing, made her laugh. Abena would often stumble over her words in Claire's presence. They were cousins and in the same grade at high school, but Claire made sure that Abena never made the mistake of thinking they could be friends.

By the time they graduated junior high, Abena's accent had softened and she was doing so well in school that Claire could no longer dismiss her as simple. In fact, had their relationship been warmer, she would have asked Abena's help with writing assignments for their English class. Here Abena excelled, due, probably, to the hours she spent alone in her room reading. Abena's braininess was the marvel of Claire's friends, who, like Claire, thought Abena *too Jamaican.* They came from comfortable homes, went to church on Sundays and showed no interest in any aspect of the Caribbean. Claire complained that reggae gave her a headache; that the smell of salt cod boiling made her want to vomit; that only people who didn't care about hygiene wore dreadlocks. She, like her mother, wore her hair straightened and lived in fear of rain or humidity. She declared that Abena, who had learned to style her hair in twists, and maintained her preference for natural hair throughout high school, did so just to be aggravating. While Claire chose a college close to home so she should could continue to live with her parents, Abena chose a college as far away from Brooklyn as possible, seeking freedom from her aunt's smothering presence and her cousin's scorn.

★

The sharp *ding* of the bell made Abena jump to her feet. Claire, punctual to the minute. The bell rang again, but still Abena did not go to the door. She was not ready for her cousin yet; she was not quite dressed. She yelled Coming! and hurried to the bedroom to rummage through a suitcase for sweatpants and a top to pull over the large, sleep-creased T-shirt she was wearing. She switched on a radio and tuned it to an r&b station, hoping the music would energize her. The blast of music filled the room, and she jogged a few steps to the beat to get herself going. But as she picked her way down the hallway through more piles of boxed-up belongings, she felt she was in the wrong apartment, in the wrong city.

Even after she'd unbolted and unlocked the front door, she paused , stretched her arms high and shook her head as though trying to dislodge lingering doubts. The doorbell rang again, for longer than before. She opened the door.

Well, that took long enough! Claire stepped into the narrow hallway. She was taller and heavier than Abena remembered. She wore jeans and a sweater under a black leather jacket. She was in full make-up. She handed Abena a plant wrapped in shiny red paper.

I've bought you a housewarming gift. She gave Abena a quick scented hug and fleeting kiss.

My, she added, not waiting for a response. She stepped past Abena into the crowded hallway and headed for the living room. There she paused, head tilted in a silent question, sniffed audibly, but did not comment on the strong marijuana smell.

Welcome home! Claire looked around at the stacks of Abena's belongings. What brings you back to Brooklyn? My goodness, all this must have cost a fortune to move! Wouldn't it have made more sense just to sell up and buy new things here rather than the cost of the packers and the movers?

Actually, no, said Abena. It didn't make sense. You know how I like to hold on to my old things. As for what brings me back: work!

The truth was, Abena had no choice but to return. The school in Albany where she had taught since graduating from college had been closed when asbestos was discovered following a fire. She was offered a temporary placement at another school on the outskirts of Albany, but she didn't like the atmosphere or its nowhere-land location. She had applied for a position at a high school in Prospect Heights without thinking too deeply about the ramifications of returning. Only now were they beginning to loom.

Abena tore off the wrapping to look at her gift. It was a mother-in-law's tongue, one of the few plants that she did not like. It used to grow like a weed in her mother's yard in Jamaica, a spiky, scratchy nuisance. She set the plant down on one of the boxes that cluttered the hall and took the jacket Claire held out to her, glancing at the designer label. Those years of training in accountancy were paying rewards.

You haven't done a thing in here! Claire stood survey-ing the stacks of boxes, arms akimbo.

Hey, I only moved in yesterday! I've hardly had time. And didn't you insist on coming to help me?

All right, all right. It looks untouched, that's all. It looks like you really do need my help. But this room – it's really nice! The place is lot better inside than it looks from the outside. So where do you want me to begin?

How about some tea first, said Abena, determined to be polite. Will mint do?

Sure, if that's all you've got.

Abena retreated to the kitchen, put water to boil, and set a tea bag and some sugar in a mug.

Do you still take it sweet? she called out to Claire, and added more sugar when Claire shouted back, Very sweet – if it's herbal.

Abena swallowed a surge of irritation. She waited in the kitchen for the water to boil, aware that she could not stop herself reacting to her cousin's expansive presence; her scent, her voice. Claire was as righteous and superior as always. This get-together was a mistake. They were cousins but that didn't mean they had to try to be friends. But that fixed, amiable smile on Claire's face as she took the mug of tea from her hands was a sign of... of what? Why had Claire contacted her, why was she visiting?

They had last met at her aunt's funeral, eighteen months before. Aunt Pinky's sudden death had left her husband immobile with grief. Claire was grief-stricken, too, but she had made all the arrangements for the funeral and the wake. Abena had taken the bus to New York to attend the funeral service, but she did not stay for the wake. She felt guilty as she made her apologies to a tearful Uncle Teddy, but he was surrounded by his relatives on the steps of the church and barely noticed her. But when she pulled Claire aside to repeat her apologies, Claire had snapped back: *Is that the best you can do? After all my mother did for you?* Abena had to admit to herself that Claire's annoyance was justified, that grudges and resentments should be buried with the dead.

While Abena was in the kitchen making tea, Claire had opened the blinds, letting in streams of sunlight that flooded through the room in dusty stripes.

It's a nice apartment, Claire said, but couldn't you have afforded two bedrooms? Then, reading annoyance in Abena's silence, she walked over to her cousin and hugged her.

I really am glad you're back, Abby. And when Abena pulled away, she added briskly: So, where to start?

Let's start in the bedroom, said Abena, pulling tape off a box crammed with clothing. If we can get things straight in there, then at least I'll sleep comfortably tonight.

The bedroom was at the back of the apartment with a window overlooking the building's interior courtyard. The room only received sunlight in the morning, but Abena liked it. A wooden dresser with an oval mirror was built into one wall and she had pushed her pine futon bed up against another. Claire moved towards the opened suitcases in the middle of the floor and the pile of hangers that lay beside them. Abena opened a carton and emptied the contents on the bed, then dragged in two extra-large, bulging black garbage bags.

Still thrift shopping, I see. Claire held up an extra large football shirt striped in red, green and yellow. And this? She held up an African print dashiki. Is this something Kofi left behind? She tossed it on the bed. What are you keeping that old thing for?

Oh, I didn't know I still had it – I should have dumped it. Abena grabbed the dashiki and threw it into a corner.

You know, I saw him on Flatbush a little while back. Have you heard from him lately?

And what do you care? You never liked him!

Claire had never shown anything but disdain for Kofi, Abena's high school boyfriend.

He wasn't my type. Claire shrugged. Anyhow, it's not that I didn't like him, she added, shaking out a sweater and then re-folding it. I just didn't think he'd be good for you.

Oh yeah? You knew him well, then?

I knew some boys like him at school. They'd be quoting Malcolm X one minute, then hiding in the toilets to smoke pot, the next. They sold that stuff in school...

Perfect little stereotypes, every one, Abena almost snarled.

When I saw Kofi the other day, he had a Japanese girl hanging on his arm... Claire paused to watch Abena's reaction.

Abena straightened up and took a deep breath. The perfume Claire wore made her head ache. She opened the window hoping the heavy, musky scent would float out and take some of the tension in the room with it. Then she grabbed an overstuffed holdall and shook its contents onto the bed, spilling an assortment of underwear in every shade of brown, from palest coffee to dark cocoa. She began to sort and fold the bras with exaggerated care.

When did you ever wear this!

Abena turned to see Claire holding up a black halternecked dress against her body. She posed in front of the mirror above the wooden dresser and stared appreciatively at her reflection. The dress was short, with a full, swirly skirt and a deep V at the front. The slippery, sinuous fabric suited Claire; her processed hair, her make-up, her shapely figure.

I've worn it to parties, said Abena. She had bought the dress on impulse just before Christmas the year before, captivated by the way it fell in soft drapes from her hips. It was expensive and buying it had made her feel extravagant and guilty, but she needed something for that special holiday party, or special date. The dress had never been worn, but she was not going to admit that to Claire.

Why don't you try it on? Abena suggested, relieved that they had found something safe to talk about. The fabric is kind of stretchy, it might fit. Go on. It'll look good, I bet.

You want to put me in a Jezebel dress? But Claire unzipped her jeans, unbuttoned her cardigan.

I bet there's someone who'd appreciate seeing you in this dress.

I'm not seeing anyone… it's been months. Claire's voice was muffled as she pulled the dress over her head.

Tell me about it! Abena didn't have to feign sympathy.

The dress clung to the curves of Claire's buttocks and moulded itself across her breasts. She turned in front of the mirror, this way and that, checking each angle.

Phew! Abena fanned herself with a hand. Hot isn't the word!

Where on earth would I wear a dress like this? It's too revealing!

Look, you're a grown woman. There's no-one's going to call down hellfire and judgement on you.

Listen to you! I'm not going to start dressing like a… Oh. You mean Mom, don't you?

Claire's voice faded. Abena saw her eyes filled with tears and felt a jolt of guilt.

No Claire, I didn't –

I know you didn't like Mom, but –

No, Claire. Aunt Pinky didn't like me!

How can you say that when she gave you a home and looked after you when you had nowhere else –

I'm not denying any of that, said Abena. I'll always be grateful to your parents for giving me a home. But that doesn't change the fact that Aunt Pinky didn't show me one jot of affection. Not once. Ever. And neither did you.

Claire reached for her handbag and pulled out a pack of Kleenex, sniffling. She blew her nose and wiped her eyes under Abena's gaze.

I've been thinking about all that… you know, since Mom died. There's a great hole in my life now… She was always there. She always had my back…

Abena heard the tremor in Claire's voice but refused to soften. What made Claire think she had time to hear her confessions? There was an apartment full of boxes to unpack. She had a new job to begin; a vast, unpredictable future awaited. So much change to negotiate.

I've only recently realized how hard it must have been for you to lose you mom so young, said Claire, almost whispering. It just didn't occur to me how hard… and you lost your home and your sister.

Abena bit her lip to push back a sudden rush of tears.

Claire moved closer to Abena and rested tentative fingers on her arm.

We didn't do a good job of comforting you, did we?

Abena shrugged off Claire's hand.

Is this why you wanted to come over; why you wanted to see me? Because *you* need comforting?

N-no. Claire's face flushed a dark brick red. I just wanted… wanted to tell you I realized I was a bitch to you when we were younger. I wanted to say I'm sorry. Now that you're back I want us to try… to make a fresh start.

Listen, Claire, I know we're cousins and everything, but I think it's too late –

Don't be so hard, Abena. It's never too late.

Well then, maybe it's too soon!

Abena went back folding clothing on the bed. Her throat felt tight, congested. She swallowed over and over, trying to dislodge the hot, dry ache. What else could she say to Claire, who slouched on the edge of her bed, quietly dabbing her eyes with a clump of tissues? She should give Claire a hug and utter forgiving words. If she could only draw from her bank of generosity and offer a kind gesture. But for the moment, the bank was closed. Abena turned her attention to putting the underthings she had folded away in drawers.

You want me to leave? Claire's voice was quiet, composed.

I think I'll do better on my own. You know what unpacking is like; it's all about sorting and finding places to put things. It's best I do it myself.

Well, if that's what you prefer... Claire stood and looked around for her purse.

Let me get your jacket, said Abena, heading for the hallway closet. Claire followed, frowning.

You know I only wanted –

It's OK, Claire. Abena forced a small smile and handed Claire her jacket. Thanks for coming to help. And thanks for the plant. I'll call you when I'm settled. We can go out for a drink or something...

Claire left with the jacket over her arm. Abena closed the door after her and leaned against it, breathing deeply, wishing she had enough weed to make another spliff. She listened until the tap tap tap of Claire's high heels faded to silence. Then she went to the living room, picked up the mother-in-law's tongue and dropped it in a box she'd set aside for garbage.

A STRIPED SILK SHIRT

The telephone rings and you jolt awake. The clock face glows in the dark: 3.40am. *Daria*, you gasp. You hear the wail of a siren, see the harried faces of a team of paramedics; an emergency room drama unfolds in front of your eyes. Your heart lurches, then drops like a stone. You reach over and grab the phone from the bedside table. Your heart thumps in your chest.

Bea? How're you doing, girl?

Your best friend's alto voice purrs in your ear, as though a 3.20 a.m. call is nothing unusual. Panic dissolves, gives way to surprise. You remember your daughter is asleep in the bedroom next to yours. You laugh out loud. It's been nearly three years since you heard from Diva and here she is, casual and easy, as though you just talked to her yesterday

Diva? Is this really you? Diva, where you been all this time?

You switch on the bedside lamp, you lean against the wicker bedhead that you bought at a Bloomingdale's sale, with Diva's help. You picture her face: earth-brown skin, copper-tinted hair, thick eyebrows that join over the bridge of her nose.

Where have I been? I thought you knew all about that. Her voice is clear, but the line crackles as though she's calling from a very long distance. The soft glow of the lamp casts shadows shaped like mountains against the bedroom walls. You wonder where she's calling from, which state, which country.

All about what? Tell me what?

Hey, I didn't call you to talk about me; I want to know what's up with you! I've been hearing some things making me worry.

You kick aside the sheet and sit up in the darkness.

About me? You been hearing things about me? Hearing things from who? What kind of things? What kind of things? Your heart starts to hammer again.

You know, I think we both need a holiday. Why don't we take some time and go visit your aunt in Jamaica? The one that lives in the hills?

I can't go away now, Diva, there's way too much going on...

I used to think that way, remember? Always too much going on. Remember?

This doesn't sound like the Diva you know. Something is different, you feel it. You reach into your memory, you strain to recall something concrete, probing and searching. Your memory has blanked, you find nothing but shadows, no trace of Diva. You break into a sweat.

Remember what, Diva?

The line crackles, and then Diva hangs up.

With the click of the telephone your eyes snap open. You are wide-awake now, your pulse is beating in your ears. You close your eyes, you lie still, you try to recapture the dream, but it is gone. You drift back into sleep.

6.50 a.m. Your clock alarms. You drag your eyelids open and force your body out of bed. Your mind is somewhere else: you recollect traces of a dream, a vague sense of anxiety. You stretch and shake yourself. You have to shower, get your daughter out of bed. You have to get dressed, get out of the house, catch the subway into the city. You have to be at your desk before 9.00 a.m., so that at 9.00 a.m. you are ready for the first phone call of the day. You long to crawl back under the sheet and recapture that drifting moment just before waking, all warmth and light, like floating on the softest cloud under the gentlest sun. Instead you teeter stork-like into the bathroom, where you peel off your sleep shirt, and push your face into the mirror to check your eyes for puffiness, your hairline for zits. In the shower you loofah your back, your elbows, the scaly skin on your heels. As you scrub, you wonder: is there a magic formula for easing gracefully into the day? How can I learn it? And the dream comes back to you.

The tepid water pumping out of the shower clears your mind: it's no effort to remember that Diva died three years ago, aged thirty-six. You believe dreams mean something. You know this dream means something. Your best friend calls you from the grave and asks you to remember the way she used to be. Why? You turn your back to the flow of water. You feel a surge of tears. Remember Diva? Who could forget her?

The first time you met her, it was New Year, and you were at a party in a Harlem brownstone. You were twenty-three, and still searching the city for the people who lived your dream of the good life. You'd gone to the party with a date you hardly knew. He left you beside the drinks table to go and check if there was anyone more interesting in the lofty rooms jammed with well-dressed, loud-talking, loud-laughing folks.

Do you know how to open a bottle of champagne without frothing it all over the place?

She wore a marbled brown panné velvet dress that hugged her body from breasts to ankles. Dreadlocks coiled across one shoulder from a knot on the crown of her head. She smiled wide and held out the dark green bottle. Your hand smoothed the back of your neatly bobbed hair and then tugged at the stretchy black skirt that fit tight across the hips. You were well dressed, looking good, but she looked better.

This is one thing I do know how to do, you said, pretending poise. You took the bottle and eased the cork gently out. You both laughed at the *pfizz* of gas, the slight spume of froth, the proof of your competence. She held out two plastic wine goblets for you to pour.

My name is Godiva, but they call me Diva. And she laughed deep in her throat.

You took the goblet in one hand, shook one of hers with the other.

I'm Bea. Happy New Year.

You came with Patrick? she asked. *Well, don't expect to see him soon.*

You know him?

Better than most. He's my brother. Good looking, isn't he?

Yes –

But no damn good! She laughed again, and took your arm and pulled you into the crowd of partymakers.

You climb out of the shower. You dry your skin, then rub oil into it. A lump the size of a walnut blocks your throat. You swallow, and swallow again, but the lump won't budge. You put away the oil and hurry out of the bathroom to rouse your daughter. Her room is filled with light: you can't figure out how she sleeps with her curtains open. She forms a hump in the centre of the bed, burrowed amid the cotton sheets like a hibernating animal, impervious to the shafts of light, to the heat of a New York summer morning; to the urgency in your voice.

Daria! You call from the doorway. She doesn't move. You are naked still, but you march up to the bed, you shake a protuberance that might be a shoulder, you try to pull back the sheet that she clutches in her sleep. You shake again. You shout: Girl, why do we have to go through this every single morning!

She moves, uncoils, uncovers her head. She blinks at you with gummy eyes, stretches a thin arm. That arm, its delicate thinness, interrupts your annoyance for one still moment. You think she's awake enough to leave her. You show your irritation with the whole performance by stomping on the floor of the passageway so the wooden floor vibrates like a muted drum. In your own room, you throw open the closet and survey the crush of skirts, pants, shirts, jackets – clothes for every mood, every occasion. You have a meeting with Patrice Voss, the vice-president, this afternoon. Your stomach clenches at thought: what is the meeting about? The fall programme? A new donor campaign? You pull out a sleeveless dress and jacket of terra-cotta linen. The tailored dress has perspiration stains at the underarm seam. You'll have to make sure not to raise your arms, or keep the jacket on, so no one will notice. You pull on sheer panty hose. The bra you usually wear with this dress is under a pile of clothing stacked on the armchair. You deliberately allow yourself few surfaces on which to dump things like clothes, underwear, magazines, reports brought home from work. You rummage among the pile of discarded clothes for the bra, resolving to put things away, to put other soiled things in the laundry. Soon.

The bedroom is large and minimally furnished: a

double bed, two bedside tables, a small TV, a dresser with a full-length mirror, an armchair covered in cream brocade, to match the walls. You stand close up to the mirror to put on your make-up. That way you avoid having to look at the bulge around your midriff, the pockets of flesh inside and outside your upper thighs. You are only too aware how fast the body deteriorates once you pass thirty-five. You are only thirty-seven and look what has happened. You are actually on a high protein diet that should take off this surplus flesh, if only you had the discipline to follow it faithfully. You still look good in clothes: you see that as soon as you step into the linen dress.

That dress got sweat stains under the arms. Your daughter leans against the doorpost, slender as a sapling, wide young-thing eyes lit by a wise-ass smile. Everyone's gonna think you don't wear deodorant.

No one's going to see, unless I walk around with my arms in the air.

You can see from the back, and it doesn't look good. She leans against the doorpost, swaying slightly and smirking. You bite your lip, annoyed at the dress, more annoyed at your daughter. You wonder when did she get so smart?

And what do you know about anything, eh miss? You better get your frowsy self into the shower, and fast!

She saunters into the room and flops on the bed. You slide out of the dress, return it to the closet and pull out a royal-blue shift with short sleeves and a matching belt. It's a little on the formal side, but maybe the meeting with Patrice Voss warrants something authoritative. The iron is by the bed. You plug it in, and while it heats, you pull your straightened, shoulder-length hair into a knot at the base of your skull.

I dreamed of Diva last night.

Oh? Daria knits her brows, like she's not sure how to respond. She knows you still miss Diva.

Was it a good dream or a bad dream?

Now it's your turn to feel uncertain. The dream made your heart pound, made you sweat. How could it be a good dream, when it made you so anxious?

Your daughter is watching you, propped on one elbow, head on hand. You lean across the bed and give her reclining body a shove.

How many times must I tell you? GET IN THE SHOWER! You place the dress on the bed and smooth it flat, ready for pressing. Daria stands watching, arms akimbo.

You got in real late last night, Mom. Kenneth shouldn't be keeping you out so late.

You glare at her so fiercely, she scampers out of the room. You feel you could smack her sassy mouth: this display of womanishness is new, and maddening. Besides, you weren't out late, you'd actually got in earlier than planned, earlier than you'd wanted. You'd wanted a long evening of pleasure with Kenneth. Once again, he'd foiled your plans. He hadn't liked the movie you'd gone to see, and insisted on leaving before the end. You left with him, and fumed all the way back to his apartment because the film, a comedy, was actually making you laugh. *It's all about standards*, he explained, as you walked from the cinema to his apartment on Prospect Place. *When we tolerate that kind of drivel, we are endorsing it.* This man, who doesn't know what a good haircut looks like, obsesses about standards. *Kenneth, it was a romantic comedy! Who takes that stuff seriously!* Kenneth is far too serious about things that don't matter. Daria once observed that he liked misery. She said he liked to see people unhappy. His pickiness, his prissiness is certainly beginning to wear out your good will. You are beginning to wonder about your daughter. She is razor sharp these days, maybe too sharp for her own good. Is that something that comes with puberty?

You iron the dress, step into it, head for the kitchen. Daria is in her room, and you know she has gone back to bed. Is she trying to provoke me you wonder as you spoon ground coffee into the coffee maker. Disobedience, feistiness, on top of everything else. The feistiness had only recently shown itself. For years after Denny left she was silent, too silent; only talking when she wanted something, or when you forced her to speak. Denny, issuing commands from the safe distance of Chicago, had wanted you to take her to a psychiatrist, but you resisted. It's a phase, you said, more from hope than knowledge. And she seemed normal in every other way. Now, she's so full of lip, she makes you uneasy. You feel a surge of annoyance at Denny. Four years now. Four years he hasn't been around to get his share of his child's more difficult moments. She is all sweetness when she sees him, and he is all pride, smiling into her eyes and calling her *princess, my cute little girl*. With you, your daughter is a foreign language that you can't translate, from an unknown country, uncharted terrain. You need time out to study her, to figure her out.

Raising a child takes two heads, Diva used to say. She never had children, and she became glad about that. At the end, when you visited her in hospital, you used to sit and hold her hand. Her form, barely visible beneath the covers, shrunk down to 70lbs. Her hair had fallen out, her beauty an old woman's: slack, ashen skin, with greenish shadows under her eyes. Daria pleaded to be taken to see her in the hospital. Diva was more like an aunt than Auntie Plummie, her real aunt that she hardly ever saw. Daria sitting by the bed with Diva's papery hand in both of hers, eyes fixed on Diva's face, stroking, stroking. *You shouldn't take the child to the hospital. You shouldn't let the child see her like that,* Mama had protested. *It will frighten her. Birth and death, two thing children shouldn't see.* Daria was only ten years old at the time, but she was not afraid. *She eases my spirit,* Diva would say, and closed her eyes while Daria stroked.

Do children understand the finality of death? You'd wanted Daria to understand that Diva was gone for ever. You took her to the funeral so she could see that Diva was in a casket, that the casket was buried in the ground. She didn't cry at the funeral. But that night, back at home, she asked: *Has Auntie Diva gone to heaven, Mom?* Those too-big eyes fixed on your face, their pupils dilated, so you knew your answer mattered. You knew your answer would make the difference between heartache and hearts-ease for your child. You didn't have the heart to say what you believed: No baby, there's no such place as heaven. You hugged her, kissed the top of her head and said: *Yes, baby, she's gone to the very best kind of heaven.* And she nodded as though she knew the answer all along.

You put Daria to bed that night and stayed with her till she fell asleep, but you didn't sleep. You didn't sleep for many nights to follow. You would lie in the dark, hearing every car that passed, every siren, no matter how distant. You would try not to think of Diva. You wanted to remember her as she had been: radiant, daring, kind. Wise, loving, sexy. But most of all, more alive than anyone you knew. She was only two years older than you. You had known that people got ill, that people died before their time. Your own father died from pneumonia, in England, when he was only forty-seven. You hardly knew him, didn't grow up with him. Maybe that was why you didn't feel the terror, the ache in your chest that you felt for Diva, when he died.

You glance at your watch: it's 8.05 a.m. How did you get to this place, rehashing ancient history, getting all upset? And what is Miss Daria doing? You gulp some coffee. You shout down the hallway.

Daria, are you in the shower yet? You listen for the sound of running water. You have to hurry, no time for that omelette you really should eat. You'll have to face Patrice Voss on an empty stomach. It wouldn't be the first time.

ii

Get out of bed! Get in the shower! Why do we have to go through this every single morning!

Yeah, why? Daria mumbles under her breath as the apartment door slams behind Bea's back. She hunches over as she dries her skin, like she's anticipating trouble, as though she feels unsafe in the bathroom, in the apartment, even though she and her mother have lived there for most of her life. She takes care to dry between her toes, relaxing a little as she dabs the pale, loose membrane joining each toe to the next. She is proud of her feet. They are baby-smooth, and perfectly straight. She would have preferred a cute face; maybe her mother wouldn't yell at her in the mornings if she had a cute face, and the kind of charm that comes easily to those who are pretty. But pretty feet are better than nothing, and look cute in their own way in strappy sandals (summer is coming), or bare, in the park, or on the sand at Riis Beach.

She's gone off in a funk again, Daria muses as she drifts back to her room to dress. That saphead Kenneth: what she see in him? She shrugs, dismissing them both. He's not worth a second of her mental energy, and her mother, well, she's just too busy, with too many problems. *There's just too much sitting on my shoulders!* Daria mimics her mother's voice. She can't see *why* Bea has all these problems. Maybe she's too young, or maybe it's because (like Bea keeps saying) she don't have enough sense. Well Daria has sense enough to read the signs. Like with Kenneth: he doesn't come over any more. Like he and Bea only see each other once a week, and not always that often. The signs were all there, and she, Daria, had already figured out that Kenneth wouldn't be around much longer.

In her small room, Daria turns on the radio and rummages in a dresser drawer for underwear. Her favourite song is playing, all bass syncopations and throaty, testosteronic vocals. *Unhuh*, the male voices chant. *Unhuhu-huhuh.* The song makes her think of boys with hungry eyes clustering around boom boxes on the stoops along Park Place and Kingston, outside buildings all around the neighbourhood. Daria pulls on some skimpy underpants and skips into the living room. She turns on Bea's hi-fi, tunes into the station playing her song and turns up the volume. The living room is a perfect space for dancing, its polished wood floor ideal for spins and turns. Daria bobs around the floor, already feeling the heat of summer, the heat in the eyes of boys on the street. She bounces like a boxer, small fists punching the air in time to the music. Her head slides from side to side, her narrow thighs, nothing but bone and muscle, her torso, a slender column, find poetry in the harsh lyrics of the song, put grace into hard, jerky steps.

There's a momentary break in the music and Daria hears old Mr Rodgers upstairs banging on the floor with his stick. Mr Rodgers is a diabetic with gangrene in his foot. He's home all day and doesn't like noise. The music resumes and the thuds on the ceiling are muffled by the song. Daria spins around the floor, her face rapt, as if she has found a place of pure pleasure. She choreographs a sequence of moves: step backwards, dip sideways, arms flying outwards in a butterfly motion. The music makes her feel like flying: all the best music makes her want to lift her arms and take off.

Daria still remembers Miss Lester, her kindergarten dance teacher, who was plump for a dancer, but she moved like a bird gliding on water, and her voice was gentle.

Imagine you are flying through sunlight! Miss Lester would turn on the tape-recording of drumming, loud drumming, that echoed in the school hall like a thousand hearts beating. The class of four-year-olds would take off, feet thundering on the floor, arms whirling like propellers. *Imagine you are a bird floating on a cloud!* Daria would twirl and spin and jump with all her might, like a young rabbit trying to take flight. Daria remembers Miss Lester, and her limbs feel light; she feels an urge to vibrate the floorboards of the mother's living room with all the power in her bony legs. The song on the radio changes, but Daria dances on until her breath gives out and she collapses, stretched out on the floor like a giant starfish, panting and grinning up at the ceiling, as though sending a message up to Mr Rodgers: Old man, this is how to start a day.

Dancing leaves Daria exhilarated and too excited to just get dressed and leave for school. English, then biology. It won't matter if she's a little late. She heads for Bea's room, where she turns on the TV and explores the dresser. There are clusters of coloured glass phials, small bottles and jars containing scent, nail lacquer, and fragrant, luxurious-looking unguents. She opens Bea's closet, which overflows with dresses, suits, shirts, blouses, sweaters. Daria fingers a black and white striped silk shirt, loving the soft feel of it. She pulls out a red suit with a narrow skirt and long tailored jacket. Too small for Bea these days, the suit is too large for Daria, but she puts it on all the same, with the silk shirt underneath. She poses hip-shot before Bea's long mirror, admiring the drape of the jacket on her thin frame, the warm colour against her skin. So easy to feel like someone else. All it takes is a change of clothes. In this suit, she feels adult and important, like she has a job, and her own office, with a cell-phone like a computer to keep track of emails and meetings and urgent deadlines. Is this how Bea feels when she's at work? Does she feel important?

Daria forgets about getting dressed for school. She finds a tube of make-up on the dresser and dabs blobs of it over cheeks and forehead, smoothing it with gentle strokes, the way the models do on TV. Eyes are circled with pencil, lips shaped into a pout, and filled in with red lipstick. Then the magic of mascara: a few strokes of the wand and Daria's eyes glow in the mirror, bright like stars in her small, dark face. She flirts in the mirror with her own reflection. A flush of pleasure spreads across her skin and she feels warm and light, like one of Bea's fluffy chocolate cakes fresh from the oven. She likes the feeling so much, she decides to wear the make-up and the shirt to school, with the close-fitting new jeans that her friend Shondra persuaded her to buy.

She wants to strut her fineness this morning, but

caution prompts her to scuttle out of the building so none of the neighbours will see her. On the street, a block away from her building, she drapes her backpack over her shoulder like an oversized purse and attempts a mannequin stride.

Daria?

Uncle Timmy's kindly eyes stare at her from the other side of the street. Daria's heart blips. She stares straight ahead, conscious of the red on her lips and the sexy cling of the shirt, knowing it's too early in the day for anyone decent to look sexy. Especially someone who's only four-teen. She keeps walking, as though she doesn't hear the dreadlocks man calling her name, over and over. Only three weeks ago, wearing Bea's long black knit skirt with the thigh-high slit, she had run into Grandma Susu on Washington. Grandma Susu hadn't said a word about the skirt. *Is a long time you haven't been over to the restaurant, chile,* she had said, offering her plump cheek for Daria's kiss. *What you so busy doing, you don't have time to visit your grandma?*

I got homework, Grandma, and stuff to do at home, you know. Grandma Susu had snorted through flared nos-trils and narrowed her eyes. That evening Bea came home snorting too. One glance at her face was enough for Daria to know that Grandma Susu had called her at the office and told her about the skirt. Daria had tried to hide in her room, but Bea ferreted her out, a leather belt in her hand. *You think you can hide from me, girl? If you think you're woman enough to wear my clothes, why run and hide like a half-sized coward? Get your skinny behind out here!* Two lashes with a thin leather belt would be a dumb way to end a day that started so sweetly. Daria stares straight ahead and marches away from her uncle.

The clock on the church down the block shows 9.30 as

Daria approaches the school entrance. She is late, but is not bothered. She is more concerned with a group of boys loitering by the heavy double doors. What will they think of the black and white silk shirt, the make-up? Will they think she looks cute? Or cheap? Or crazy? With a small intake of breath she recognizes Alphonse Passat and his cronies – Tomas, Guy, and Claud-Pierre, known as Ci-Pi. Alphonse and his friends are only juniors, but Alphonse is tall, and built like he spends his afternoons working out. He stands slightly apart from the other three, his weight on one foot, one hand buried in the back pocket of his over-sized jeans, the other holding aloft a fat, hand-rolled cigarette.

Daria walks past, trying with all her strength to keep her head high. She feels Alphonse's gaze like a blowtorch against her skin. A flush rises up her back, over her face, so hot that perspiration prickles at the edge of her scalp. She is all too aware of her nipples, as hard as dried peas, under the thin silk of her mother's shirt. Alphonse calls out something she doesn't understand – what is the language these Haitians speak? – and the other boys laugh. Daria wishes she had Shondra's quick tongue or, better still, a mouth like Petal's, the new girl in class, fresh from Jamaica and talking *raw chaw* patois. Petal had already bested Alphonse in a quick-fire curse fight, following a brief skirmish by a classroom door. The whole school was talking about it. Petal had unintentionally jostled Alphonse. Alphonse had blocked the doorway so she couldn't pass; Petal had called him an ignorant animal. *You need some time with me, bitch*, he'd said, thinking he'd had the last word. *I'll show you what that tongue is for. Oh yes?* Petal had retorted. *You want me to bite it off?* And she'd shoved him with her hip and pushed her way into the classroom.

Daria has no mouth, no skill at wounding with words. No way to defend herself against a boy like Alphonse. She caves in under his gaze, hunches her shoulders and scuttles through the door.

She is half an hour late for the English class, but the teacher, Mr Parrish, only rolls his eyes as she hurries to the vacant desk beside Shondra, who always occupies a corner at the back of any classroom.

Where you be going so late? Shondra whispers.

Daria rolls her eyes like Mr Parrish, and shrugs.

Well, wherever it be, you sure worked up a sweat. And what you wearin? You think you look cute or somethin?

Shondra is looking more than cute in baggy jeans and a white t-shirt with the neck scooped just low enough to show the slight swell of her breasts. Braided extensions frame her face, hanging past her shoulders. She is two months younger than Daria, but her face looks five years older. Sparkly blue shadow frosts her upper eyelids, but it's the wary tilt of her chin, and tautness in her stocky physique that suggests knowingness.

Ran into that bug Alphonse outside, whispers Daria, digging into her backpack for her notebook and a cover-less copy of Romeo and Juliet.

Easy now. He's a tad on the grown side for you.

You wouldn't catch me with his funky ass!

You two at the back! Mr Parrish is staring in their direction. What is the cause of Tybalt's duel with Mercutio?

Some kind of family argument? Shondra actually likes Shakespeare.

Hmm, yes. A little less whispering back there, please.

I was only telling Daria where we were at, Mr Parrish. And Daria opens her textbook and holds it up for Mr Parrish, as if to show him that she really is an attentive student. Mr Parrish rolls his eyes.

Daria and Shondra were in the same class at elementary school, but they were not friends then. They exchanged no more than a few words in all the years of being in a classroom together. Daria was seven when Shondra joined the school, and even then she was nervous of Shondra's ability to start fights with girls bigger than herself, fights that she would always win. She was short for her age, but she was tough, and mean when provoked. Shondra was barely aware of Daria's existence; she had none of the qualities Shondra admired in a girl: she wasn't fly, and if she was tough, it didn't show. Shondra took in Daria's unfocused gaze, her tendency to gaze out of the window during class, and decided she was dumb. Even if she wasn't dumb, Shondra decided, she looked dumb. Even worse, Daria had once been caught sucking her thumb in class. After that episode, if Shondra thought of Daria at all, she thought of her as a big, dumb baby.

Their friendship began the afternoon they were both due to graduate. Minutes before the ceremony began, Daria found Shondra in the washroom bent over a sink, the taps turned on full, jets of water splashing loud against the enamel basin, but not loud enough to drown the sound of Shondra sobbing.

Somethin the matter? Daria was unsure of how to address Shondra. She thought tough girls didn't cry, but there she was, the toughest girl in the school, crying her heart out. Daria approached and put a hand on Shondra's shoulder.

Something the matter? She'd whispered again. Shondra shrugged the hand away without looking to see whose hand it was. She continued to sob. Daria hesitated. She couldn't think of anything to say, and didn't want to risk another touch. Should she leave Shondra alone? She found it hard to turn away from a girl in distress. Instead of leaving, she fetched two paper towels from the dispenser and offered them to Shondra.

Here, she said, then watched in silence as Shondra splashed her face with water, then blotted her face with the coarse, brownish paper.

I suppose your Mom and Dad are out there, waiting to see their baby... A sob muffled Shondra's words.

No they ain't. Daria's voice was steady, her tone quiet. *My Mom's at work and my Dad's in Detroit.* She thought it best not to mention Granma Susu and Aunt Pearline, who had come as Bea's substitutes. *Your Mom can't come either?*

The whole class knew that Shondra's dad wasn't around. The whole class knew that Shondra's mom had some kind of problem: crack, or aids, something serious. Even before Daria had heard the gossip about Shondra's family, she could tell from the hard expression that sometimes settled on Shondra's face and from her restless, searching gaze, that she'd never been Daddy's special baby girl, or Mommy's either.

Darius's mom ain't coming. Nor Antonio's. Daria shrugged casually. *Ain't no big deal, anyway.*

Shondra's wary eyes searched Daria's face for any trace of sarcasm or levity.

Daria shrugged again, and returned stare for stare. Shondra drew a deep breath and released it in a long whistling sigh, as though exhaling away the thing that had gripped her heart and caused the tears.

O.K., she said, bracing herself. *C'mon, let's get it over with*.

Daria followed Shondra out of the washroom, a satisfied gleam in her eyes.

★

By the end of the day, there is no trace of Daria's morning glow. The lipstick is no more than a pinkish tint, the eyeliner a tired, dark smudge. Half an hour before the end of school, Daria's belly begins to knot. She's used to the feeling, like an invisible hand has reached inside and taken a fierce grip of her intestines. The feeling begins every day at the same time, and every day Daria takes the griping in her guts as a signal to plot her escape from the dangers waiting outside the school door: the crush of bodies, the shouting, the name-calling. The fist fights, the knife fights, the girls' fights. As if getting to school in the morning isn't hard enough, you had to fight your way out again at the end of the day. Daria's exit strategy is to rush out as soon as the last class is over. If the last class runs over time, she tries to leave with Shondra, or Petal, or someone who can defend themselves and, if necessary, her as well.

Her last class is history, and the teacher runs over by eleven minutes. Daria begins to pack up her books as soon as the bell sounds. When the class is dismissed, she rushes for the door, jostling her classmates, who are also rushing to get out. Down by the lockers, she cranes her neck looking for Shondra, who is nowhere in sight, nor Petal either. She shrugs on her backpack, forgetting its worn edges and the fragile silk shirt. She grips the straps tight, each hand forming a fist, each fist resting on a rib. She hunches her shoulders, drops her head and marches forward, like a timid soldier heading into a fray.

Adolescent bodies of all shapes and sizes stampede their way out of the school building, their collective voices raised in a strident babble of wordless noise. In the open air, they crowd the sidewalk in clumps. Daria has to edge her way along, one shoulder leading, in order to avoid bumping into somebody or brushing somebody with her backpack, and calling down a torrent of insults. Once, she had inadvertently kicked the anklebone of an older girl who in a second was pummeling Daria's cringing body with blows. She had been rescued that time by her cousin Kriss whose arrival, at the precise moment she most needed him, had seemed like a miracle. Kriss, a senior and an athlete, tall and sinewy, a long distance runner. He had reached out and taken a handful of Daria's assailant's hair and pulled her away. Then, with his arm around her, he had led Daria though the gawping crowd, which parted in awe to let them through.

Daria thinks fleetingly of Kriss as she inches her way along the block. He is Uncle Timmy's son. He is quiet, soft spoken and kind – as kind as Uncle Timmy. In the fall, he will be moving away to a sporting college in Connecticut. Another person gone, she is thinking, when she hears a voice calling her name.

Yo, Daria! Dah-ree-ah!

Daria starts, and looks around. She is halfway down the block, and the crowd is still thick. She feels a tap on her shoulder, and starts again.

Ah – oh! she stammers. Alphonse is smiling down at her. His smile is wide, revealing a gold tooth just off centre. The tooth gleams hard and bright; it distracts Daria's attention from the glitter in his eyes. He throws an arm around her shoulder, and once again Daria witnesses the parting of the throng.

You sure look cute today, Daria. You know that? Alphonse sounds mild, affable, like an older brother, but the arm around her shoulder makes her uneasy.

Like a grown woman in that shirt, that lipstick. How come I never noticed you before?

A tremor ripples down her spine, her tongue freezes.

What is she supposed to say? Tell him the shirt is her mother's? That she has to hurry home and take it off? Part of her wants to run, to get away from the weight of his arm on her shoulder, the glittery smile. The other part of her, the part that wants to explore, to discover, to know, looks up at him, forces a smile and stammers:

It's n-new. My mom g-gave it to me.

Let me carry your pack, he suggests, and straight away begins to ease the straps off her shoulders. Which way you walkin?

Huhh? Is this happening? To me, Daria?

Feel like a stroll in the park? That smile, that glimmer of gold.

A spark of fear in her belly. A flare of excitement in her chest. Daria glances at his face, flushes when he meets her gaze, then stares down at the granite sidewalk. They walk towards the Parkway and stop. A left turn leads eventually to Daria's building, a right turn to the park. Daria freezes, heart thumping against her ribs, unable to decide which way she wants to go.

I know a cool spot in the park, near the lake. We can sit and watch the ducks.

She looks at his face. He looks back at her with an indulgent half-smile. She hears the roar of traffic, which is loud all of a sudden, as though by general consensus all the cars on the road are revving their engines. She feels a trickle of perspiration running down each side from her underarms. It is hot for the time of day, for June. Summer is already here. That thought surfaces and echoes like an insistent whisper in her head. The lake, cool, clear as glass. Her favourite part of the park.

O.K., she says.

His arm slides from her shoulder. His hand takes hold of her arm. They turn right onto Eastern Parkway and Alphonse's stride begins to lengthen. Daria opens her mouth to complain that he's walking too fast, but she shuts it again, not wanting to sound like a whiner or a wimp. Maybe they will run into Granma Susu, or Uncle Mikey. Maybe she should have left school with Shondra.

Once inside the park, Alphonse slows down and Daria's heartbeat settles, soothed by the cool scent of grass and earth and leaves. They leave the road and head across Long Meadow in the direction of the lake. There are people scattered over the meadow: women playing with toddlers, old people resting on benches watching the women and their young. A rastaman is playing Frisbee with four dreadlocked children. He throws the disc to each in turn. Each child catches it and throws it back, wildly, so the man has to run to retrieve it, his long dreadlocks swinging like a veil of blackish rope.

They pass a pair of lovers leaning against a tree, kissing deeply. Daria's heart lurches, not in fear this time, but excitement deeper than any she can remember.

She knows what is coming and she thinks she knows what to do. Shondra had prepared her. Shondra had done it all: kissed and been kissed, fondled, and fondled in return. She'd had sex: sex in a bed, sex in this same park. Daria knew all the boys' names, all the details. She knew, too, that Shondra despised her inexperience as the most serious sign of dumbness. *Aint no big deal. Is something everybody gotta do, 'cept nuns, and freaks with hang-ups. Don't know what you waitin on.*

Bea had talked to her about periods and intercourse and babies, but that was different, like a personal biology lesson. Bea had told her to wait; to wait for maturity, to wait for privacy, for love. *Too much teenage sex going on, too many teenage pregnancies.* None of Bea's advice even flickered in Daria's mind. None of it had anything to do with making out with a cute boy in the park.

The walk to the lake is taking an age. Alphonse's body knocks against hers as they walk, his arm is around her, yet his eyes roam the park and linger on each pretty girl they see. The march across the grass begins to feel like a drag and the silence dampens her excitement. Daria feels to say something, to start a conversation and bring his eyes back to her again.

Uh… is there time to walk all the way to the lake?

In a hurry or something? Narrowed eyes, no smile.

No. Just my legs getting tired. All that walking, you know.

Don't have to go as far as the lake. Matter fact, I know a real quiet spot, just over there. He points to a hillock topped with a clump of wide-spreading trees, some twenty yards on. Matter fact, you can see the lake from there. Cool?

There's quiet within the circle of trees that feels like they are in a private place, a garden or a secluded wood. Alphonse drops Daria's backpack by a tree-trunk and sits on the grass beside it. Daria stretches on tiptoe, shading her eyes with one hand, looking towards the silver-green glimmer of the lake.

Can't see no ducks, she says.

Fuck the ducks! says Alphonse. He grabs her arm and pulls her down beside him. He leans over and pushes a hand under her shirt. His fingers crawl up her torso, feeling for a breast. He finds it, and squeezes her nipple.

Ow! That hurts!

That's s'posed to feel good. What's wrong with you, girl?

He pulls her against him with his free hand and presses his mouth on hers. He squeezes with his fingers, crushes with his lips. Daria can't breathe. She tries to pull away, but his arm is clamped around her. His tongue pushes against her teeth. She struggles to draw a breath, thinking: Nobody said anything about suffocation. An instinct tells her to stop wriggling. She parts her teeth and takes in a gulp of air with Alphonse's tongue. It feels fat and slippery in her mouth, like a quick, darting fish.

His hand leaves her nipple to tug at the zip on her jeans. Her squeal of protest is muffled by his tongue. She summons all her strength and pushes his hand away with both of hers.

You got your period?

She nods, breathing fast, almost panting.

You touch me, then. He fumbles with his belt, unzips his jeans and pushes her hand inside his boxers.

She is startled by the way it stirs against her fingers. She giggles, nervous.

Squeeze it, he commands.

She obeys, and it grows even harder in her hand. He pushes the shorts down over his hips so he can see, so she can see it, purplish, veiny and hard.

Wanna make me a very happy man today?

He puts a hand behind her head and pushes it down to his crotch. Take it in your mouth, he says.

She doesn't mind the musty taste: it tastes the way the earth, the twigs, the fallen leaves they are sitting on smell. She touches it with her tongue, and it leaps in her mouth, a bigger fish. He groans and jerks upwards with his pelvis, at the same time his hand pushes her head down. It rams against the back of her throat and she gags. She gags again and her whole body convulses in a surge of panic. She bites. He shrieks, and rams his fist against her head.

Fukinssstupidmuthfukinho! Dumbstupidpissassho!

He struggles to his knees, holding his penis with both hands. Daria's head is shot with pain. She is too dazed to realize she should get up and run. He staggers to his feet, vomiting curses. He pulls up his jeans and aims another blow at her head. His fist lands against her cheek, crunching a corner of her mouth against the teeth beneath.

You stink, bitch! Fuckincrazydumb bitch!

He kicks out, but Daria turns away so the toe of his boot lands against a rib. She screams in pain and rolls over on the ground. He buckles his pants and staggers away, holding his crotch. He leaves Daria doubled-up on the ground. She is sobbing. Her cut mouth is bleeding. She tastes tears and blood, salt and metal, and sobs even harder.

iii

Weariness weighs on your shoulders as you turn the key in the door. You kick off your shoes as soon as you step inside, and your feet seem to heave their own sigh of relief. You call to your daughter: Honey, I'm home! She calls out in reply, saying what you can't tell for the music playing loud in her room. She has cleared up the kitchen. You have trained her to do this, but more times than not, she forgets, so it comes as a pleasing surprise when she does it. She has taken a chicken from the freezer to defrost. She has cleaned and washed a measure of white rice and set it to soak like a trove of seed pearls in cloudy water. If she hadn't done these things, you would be banging on her door, complaining that you are not her cook and housekeeper. How many times, how many evenings have been ruined in this way. You do not need that particular stress this evening; you have eaten nothing but a bagel all day and you sat for two hours in a meeting with the Vice President, your belly growling while he chattered on and on about the fall donation collection programme. All day long you have felt hot and sweaty in a too-fitted dress. Summer has taken you by surprise.

Your skin relaxes when you peel off the royal blue dress. You wonder why you keep it: it's ill fitting, and that particular shade of blue makes your complexion look ashy. You keep it because you have the habit of thrift, learned from your mother. She owns a restaurant and two brownstones, yet cuts pantyhose in half to save the undamaged leg. *Waste it*, she'd say, *and you'll soon want for it*.

You shower, and rest for a few minutes. You lie down in your underwear, then remember to check your messages. Only one, from Denny. He's moving back to the city in August. A great job offer. Hmm. Good news for Daria... maybe. You don't want to think about Denny now. You lie down and try to doze, but your thoughts keep racing, racing. The half-year accounts. The summer fundraising targets. Patrick Voss flashing his quick smile. Why does it make you uneasy? No one else in the office smiles at you, except Jannine, the payroll clerk, and she smiles at everyone. You've gotten used to indifference. Your new assistant, Terence, still not pulling his weight. Maybe fifty-eight really is too old. Seems diligent, always poring over some document, works late most evenings. So why aren't the figures for June ready? Patrick will blame you for the delay. He'll wrinkle his forehead and look concerned, and say, *How are you coping, Bea?* You need to have a word with Terence... Kenneth didn't call. Must be mad about last night. Didn't really quarrel over that movie... more of a disagreement. Can't argue with him the way you could with… Always, it's his manhood at stake, even in a silly tiff about a movie. What a burden. What a burden to have to pander to his… You have one child already.

You realise you haven't seen your daughter since you came home. What's she doing in her room? Loud music, no hug. No *hi mom*. Oh. Oho.

You get up and pull on your robe. You pad down the hall, you knock on her door.

Daria! If you'd turn down that noise, you'd hear me knocking!

The volume decreases. You listen for her to call you in. The call doesn't come. You push open the door, you walk in. She is lying on the bed, her face turned to the wall. You could think she's sleeping, but her limbs are too neatly placed, legs together and fully stretched out, hands together and under her cheek. Like she was praying and drifted into sleep. You know she's only pretending. You think perhaps she's playing with you, that she will spring up lioness-style when you get close, one of her favourite little games when she was small that she still plays occasionally, when in high spirits. You tiptoe to the bed, you pretend you don't realize she can hear you. You pounce, grab her shoulder, and roll her over. You see her face, and your mouth drops open. The purple eye, the swollen cheek, the swollen, broken lip.

Ohmygod! Who did this?

Your heart thuds, your fingers curl into claws.

What happened to you, Daria? Who did this!

You sit beside her and make your voice sound calm. She pulls the sheet over her head, but you pull it back. You place your hand on the undamaged cheek and turn her face towards you, gently.

I got into a fight. So low, you can barely hear.

With who? About what? It's not like you to fight! Where did it happen?

On… on the way home from school. Some girl picked on me for no reason.

Picked on you for no reason? What kind of fucking animals do they have at that school?

Don't swear, Mom.

What's her name, this girl? Is she bigger than you? She sits up, then gasps and clutches her side. You push away her hands, lift up her t-shirt to look. You see a bruise that arcs like a small banana to the side of her rib cage, a few inches below her left breast.

We're going to the emergency room. Now!

Aw no, Mom. It'll be better tomorrow…

She might have broken your rib! Look how you're wincing! You're in pain. C'mon, miss, get your clothes on. And tomorrow morning, we're going up to that school and I'm going to make sure that girl gets suspended!

You don't call your Mom till you get back from the hospital, because you don't want her to worry. Your skinny little daughter, all beaten up, like some street ruffian.

Except a ruffian would have had some anger, some rage against her assailant, not this shrinking, almost guilty timidity. In your wild mind you are storming into the principal's office, confronting her with your daughter's injuries. You are demanding punitive action against that girl, the animal. Another voice, your calm mind, is reasoning: What can you do now? It happened. Not your fault, you can't prevent what you didn't forsee.

You make her comfortable on the sofa. Open windows, turn on a fan, the TV. You warm some milk, add vanilla and honey, the way she likes it. You give it to her with a straw. You start to make dinner, but the defrosted chicken reminds you of a newborn, legs and arms all curled up. It looks vulnerable. Your eyes mist over.

You remember that you didn't plan to have her. You didn't even *want* to have her, at first. She came out of nothing more than a flicker of everyday desire, a moment of routine pleasure. You weren't even in love with Denny then. *Didn't you take precautions?* your sister asked, adding irresponsibility to her list of your failings. *Are you sure you want to do this?* Denny had asked. Meaning, are you sure you won't have an abortion; I'm not ready for fatherhood yet. *Are you sure you're ready for this?* your mother asked. You had been afraid to tell her. You were afraid of her disappointment, afraid of what you might read in her eyes. She touched your cheek with a nervous hand. She is a capable woman: short, but *talawa*. Tough. Strong. Her hand does not shake easily. You knew from the tremor of the veined, beringed fingers that she feared for you. Later, as your belly grew, you recalled the trembling hand, and you wondered then, as you do now, did she carry you fearfully in her womb?

Mom? You got a moment?

The restaurant full tonight, she says. Voices hum in the background, the bell-like chink of cutlery rattling.

It's Daria.

What happen...?

Nothing to panic about... a bully picked on her, a girl at school... bruised her ribs and cut her lip.

Children not even safe at school these days. She clucks deep in her throat.

I'm going to see the principal about it in the morning.

I'll come with you. What time?
Nine? I'll come for you.

It was a marvel how she came. She came out of nothing and she took over your life. Just when you got used to her turning and turning inside you, in a world you could only see on a sonogram, she forced her way out, into your world. She tore your flesh. She stole what privacy you had. Your belly was marked by her, your whole body changed. You body was no longer your own; your body belonged to her, her nourishment, her haven. You felt she was yours, yours alone. Cradling her the first time, new and almost weightless in your arms, you trembled. You ached at the sight of delicate dark eyelids, purple rosebud mouth. She squirmed in your arms, murmuring. You broke out in sweat, your knees trembled, remembering: the beating in your womb, the second heart.

You read somewhere that if an infant loses sight of its mother for more than two or so hours, the infant imagines the mother is dead and begins to mourn. The child feels all the pain and heartbreak of loss. Every morning when you left your daughter with her childminder, Marianna, you rained kisses on her head, you murmured assurances. At lunchtime you would wonder what pictures were running through her mind, what she was feeling. If she were crying for you, grief stricken. Her joy when you collected her at the end of the day, the frenzy of squeals as you walked through Marianna's front door. Were they expressions of relief at your miraculous return to life? You told yourself she was learning early about separation: that parting need not mean the end of a thing; that parting holds the promise of return.

When you were fourteen, Daria's age, you lived with

your Aunt Martha in Jamaica. You, your sister Plummie, your brother Baltimore. Your mother was in New York, your father lived with his new woman in Kingston. Aunt Martha's house was small, wooden, damp in the rainy season. It perched like a birdhouse on a hillside. For years you lived for your mother's fortnightly letters. You didn't see her from you were nine till you were sixteen.

Your father called today.
   Uh huh? Daria is staring out the window at the sky.
   He left a message. Says he's moving back to New York. In August.
   Your daughter looks at you, disbelief in her eyes, mouth fixed by its dressing in a downturn, like a sneer.
   Sure you didn't dream it?
   What d'you mean?
   You dreamed Auntie Diva called you, remember? There she goes; Miss Smart-ass again.
   Yeah, well this is a real message on my very real answering machine. I thought you'd be pleased –
   I'll be pleased when I see him.

A Saturday morning in January. Sunlight glancing off crystalline snow on the ground. Daria was excited by the snow, the first fall of the winter. A new TV, thirty-six inches wide, dominated a corner of the living room. You'd bought it for Denny for Christmas, as though a larger TV might keep him home, keep him from leaving. Not knowing this, Daria had been excited about the TV's size, about the prospect of watching sports or movies together with her father on this giant, mesmerizing screen.
   You went to fetch her from her room. She came, already quiet. Perhaps she read something in your eyes, or

maybe it was in her father's face, because she started to cry as soon as he took her hand. You both told her, each of you holding a hand. Denny actually spoke the words, you'd insisted on that. It was his turn to do the dirty family work. He didn't shirk this time.

But why you gotta leave, Daddy?

He looked at the ceiling, looked through the window at the sky.

Don't you love me any more?

Baby, this is about me and your mom, not you. He held her against him while she sobbed. His eyes teared and so did yours. You both wept for the pain you had brought to our daughter.

After Denny moved out, Daria cried herself to sleep at nights. Night after night, week after week. You would go to her room, try to hold her and give comfort, but she would move away and huddle at the far side of the bed, against the wall. You would talk to her, try to explain that adults sometimes can't get along; that Daddy would be there for her whenever she needed him. You disbelieved yourself as you spoke, and you knew she didn't believe you. Less then a year later Denny moved to Detroit and Daria stopped speaking. She would say *yes* or *no*, but nothing more for almost a month. You could see she blamed you, not her father, for the break-up. She was angry with you.

Daria lies immobile on the sofa, staring out of the window, seeing what out there? You search her profile trying to guess her thoughts, but you have no clues, no guide. Smart-ass one moment, air-head the next. There was a time her habit of retreating into her own world alarmed you. You thought of attention deficit, autism. But she made reasonable progress at school, and you saw there was nothing wrong with her ability to think, to reason. Just this switching off, this drifting away. Even now, as you watch her, you feel she is not really in the room with you. Your mother always said she would grow out of it. She said what you would expect your mother to say: *Daria need a baby brother or sister, and a father figure around the place.* The problem, your mother says, is that she *spoil* and *self-ish*. Words your mother speaks as though they describe cardinal sins, or criminal tendencies. Which they are in the world your mother comes from, the island community in which you were born.

You did not want to raise your child as you were raised. You wanted her to be a free child; free to play, laugh, feel. Free to be a child. You didn't want to make her your domestic helper, overburdened with chores and responsibilities. Back home, when you were still a child, you had to mind your sister Plummie. You were only three years older, but she was your responsibility. When you were ten, you washed her clothes, you combed her hair, made sure she was neat and clean on schooldays before you took care of yourself. Baltimore, the eldest, had different tasks, being a boy. Fetching water from the tank, coal for the stove. Clearing the yard, back and front and helping Aunt Martha in her lean-to shop.

Your mother sent for you all. She brought you to live with her here in Brooklyn. Eventually. The girls first, then eventually Baltimore. When you were in Jamaica, fretting over the homework you had to do, and the schoolwork you couldn't finish, you dreamed of America. You never dreamed life here could be so hard. Different, strange, but not hard. Plummie always preferred Jamaica; she moved back there five years ago. She has a husband and a child of her own now. When she recalls the years with Aunt Martha, does she remember how you cared for her? She has a child of her own now, so she must know. The burden of it. The weight of a young life on your hands.

TALKING TO STRANGERS

I awake to the late spring morning still in the grip of a dream. I lie still for a while, sensing the unfamiliar contours of my new bedroom: the moulded walls, the built-in closet, the sturdy panelled door. The solidity of the walls and the furniture is comforting, but not enough to dispel the lingering sensations of the dream. I still feel as if my legs are on fire. You know the sensation: being half in the world of real things and half caught up in the drama of dreaming.

I sleep with the curtains open so when I awake, the light will dissipate traces of sleep. When I sit up I realise my skin is slick with sweat. My head spins, and when I swallow, the tissues of my throat rasp. I touch my neck, feeling for swollen glands. Just then the living room radiator glugs like a great thirsty gullet, explaining the near-tropical heat in the room, the dryness of my throat, even the dream. The cool blue sky that I can see from my bed tempts me to get up, invites me outside. I roll out of bed, wash, dress and, thirty minutes later, I step out of my front door.

Mr Brown, the super, is sweeping the lobby, as he does every morning, meticulously, as though he were the proud owner of the building. He nods slightly in my direction without disturbing his concentration on the dust accumulating at his feet. I am a newcomer and worse, a foreigner. I haven't earned his attention yet.

Mr Brown, the heating is on too high in the building.

So watcha expect me to do, eh? He stops sweeping to turn uninterested bulldog eyes on me.

How about adjusting the thermostat?

Is that what you do where you come from? Ask God to turn it down when it gets too hot? Haha!

He chortles into the overgrown hairs of his moustache. This morning, as on many other mornings before, I sense his resentment. Most of the tenants in the building are black, like him, but he seems to have no sense of fraternity with us, maybe because many of us are foreign, from the Caribbean. It piques me that he has never let me charm a smile out of him. I sense his bulldog gaze boring into my back as I stride out of the building and allow the doors to slam.

The solitary trip to the Promenade early on Saturday morning is one of my favourite things to do, and every time it feels like a treat, a small adventure. I take a short cut through the Botanic Gardens, and catch the 41 bus to Court Street. There's only a trickle of traffic on the streets and when I walk down Montague Street it's quiet, almost peaceful. Its shuttered storefronts look like sleeping eyes; only the coffee shop and neighbouring bakery are open. I stop to pick up a cappuccino and a warm cinnamon bagel. This walk, the aroma of the coffee and the warmth of the bagel in my hand are a ritual I have created to make myself feel part of this place.

Down by the river the air stings my face. In the distance, the sky over Manhattan is a pale blue and below the Promenade sunlight shimmers on the surface of the water. I stop by a slatted bench, one of a long row facing the river, and set down my coffee before easing in and throwing back my head to catch some sun on my face. I glance towards the Manhattan shore, remembering the Twin Towers and the way their windows used to glisten and dazzle, light igniting glass so the buildings seemed vibrant, alive.

The blue of the sky and the glancing sunlight calls to mind the luminous blue of sky and sea back home. A wave of homesickness as fierce as hunger engulfs me. I loll back on the bench, prepared to travel in my mind. But a man approaches, noiselessly, and looms beside me for an instant, then drops his weight on the neighbouring bench, exhaling loudly through his nostrils, like a horse. He has hair the colour of dried grass and a neat pattern of crow's feet around his eyes. He wears a light jacket and black sweat pants, and a thin, silver hoop in one ear. I glare at him, hoping he will feel embarrassed enough to move to one of the many vacant benches further along the Promenade. But he settles his paper cup of coffee on the seat and unfolds his newspaper. He either ignores, or fails to notice my unwelcoming gaze.

When he looks up, I look away. I feel his glance travelling, taking in my posture, my hair, the fit of my jeans. A warm, slightly unpleasant feeling rises at the back of my neck as his gaze hovers. I sense that he's speculating on the shape of my breasts. I look sharply at him and his eyelids droop. I can tell he's thinking of sex.

But maybe not. Maybe I'm wrong. Maybe he only sees a youngish black woman with tan skin and low-cropped hair and doesn't notice her shapely figure. Perhaps she barely registers in his mind. And if she does, perhaps he's thinking that she's from around here, maybe a clerk in one of the shops on Montague Street having breakfast. If he's perceptive (in a way that few men are), he might sense that she is Caribbean. He might place her as a domestic worker or a nanny, someone who minds the children of one of the wealthy, white, professional couples who live in the elegant buildings whose ornate rear windows overlook the benches where we sit. But he is probably thinking none of this; he probably hasn't given me a second thought.

A sudden sound like someone choking makes me look at him again. The man is rocking gently, not choking but laughing, head buried between the pages of his paper, which quivers in time with his muffled *haw haws*. His mirth is invasive, a violation of my sombre mood. I clear my throat and scowl.

He lowers the paper, still laughing.

I was just scanning the personals, he says, ignoring my frown. Some of these ads are so pathetic, I'd cry if I didn't laugh. Listen to this: *Beautiful, brilliant, athletic woman, mid-fifties, seeking youthful partner for fun, love, maybe more.* You'd think by her age she'd know better!

He is forcing me out of my world, into his. I decide not to resist.

My Aunt Susan married her second husband at fifty-eight, I say.

They didn't meet through a personal ad, I'm sure, he says.

They met at church…

You see my point?

Not really…

So you think you can find love by advertising for it?

It's too early for such a question, for such a conversation with a stranger. Just to think about this question could set off a train of thought that would crash into memories, into my personal heap of disappointments. Suddenly, the memory of the morning's dream surfaces so strongly my heart jumps. In the dream I am running from a moving wall of fire that shoots out tongues of flame. The flames circle my legs, their heat softly licking my calves. I am sprinting, panting like a marathon runner, but the flames catch up with me, engulfing my legs. In remembering, I relive the feeling of panic and my breath runs short. I am trapped once again, between the realness of the Promenade, the bench and the man, and the other world of the dream.

The man looks at me, and I see him wondering: Is she O.K.? Is she crazy? Out here alone so early in the morning, there are so many weirdos in this city and most of them look as normal as she does.

I hope I haven't touched a nerve, he says. Some people don't like to talk about love.

You're right about that, I say. It's too complicated a subject to discuss first thing in the morning.

With a stranger, I think but do not say. Instead, I tell him something my father once said.

My father only visited New York once and only for nine days, but he said the city was a loveless place. There was everything here to ignite love, he said, but nothing to nurture it. He said it was a place without a heart.

I see your father thinks he is an expert on love, the man says.

My parents have been married for forty-three years, I say, as though this is relevant.

And perhaps it is. My parents seem to have a happy marriage. If you were to see them, you would think they are a loving couple. My father is the more demonstrative one: *Forty-three years together, and I don't regret a single day*, he will say whenever the subject of marriage arises in conversation. My mother agrees in his presence, but once, long ago, I overheard her talking with my aunt on the veranda – the same aunt who married her second husband at fifty-eight – and I heard my mother sigh, *Ah, chile, what can I tell you? Married life is…* I couldn't catch the rest, the words that pronounced her judgement on marriage, but I've never forgotten the hushed, incompleteness of it and the sigh that preceded it. That sigh made me doubt that my mother thinks my father is an expert on love.

My parents live in the same town where they were born and grew up. In the 1960s they left the town, left the island, to seek their fortunes in London. They returned to the same town in the early 1990s, after their children had left home and after my father retired from his job on London Transport with a pension paid in pounds that was almost worth a fortune in Jamaican currency. At the very moment that I'm being drawn into conversation with this stranger, they'd be sitting on the tree-shaded verandah of their recently-build house, breakfasting on calalloo with fried dumplings, and scalding, bitter-sweet coffee. They'd be conversing in leisurely murmurs, planning the day's activities, the day's meals, and wondering how their daughter in New York is doing. I wish myself on the verandah with them. I see Mama setting a place at the wicker breakfast table, pouring coffee, sweetening it with condensed milk, the way I love it, Pops reaching across the table to pat my hand and ask in his quiet voice, *Is everything alright with you, pumpkin?* I see myself striving to enter their intimacy, searching for words to make them think I'm as happy as they are, that I'm as satisfied with life – searching for words they would believe. *I love my new apartment, Pops*, is all I can think to say, even in this daydream.

You look as though you're some place far away. The man once again demands my attention.

I was thinking of my parents.

And where are they?

They live in the Caribbean.

Mmm, he says. Nice. So what brought you to America?

My eyes follow the movement of boats on the river. Two police launches come chugging into view and pass each other, leaving parallel white ribbons of foam in their wake. My gaze shifts to a sailboat heading seaward, while I search for a flippant answer.

Oh, I'm just another immigrant, I say, and he nods, missing, I'm sure, the irony.

Me too, he says, and then adds: Though maybe migrant would be a more appropriate word.

Migrant, immigrant. I suppose we're all running away from something, I say. He nods again.

Or towards something, he says.

A woman comes teetering by, pulled at the end of a leash by a dog, a large Labrador with a luxuriant blonde coat. The woman wears jeans and a sweater and walks with hipbones thrust forward. She strides like a model, but her attempt at a runway glide is sabotaged by the dog's brisk trot. She has pale skin and pale, glossed lips, hair that swings around her shoulders. The man eyes her, his lips slightly parted.

Nice dog, he says, loud enough for the woman to hear as she staggers past the bench. He follows her progress with his gaze. New York is still a wonderful place, he adds beneath his breath.

My first visit to the Promenade was on the fourth of July, two years ago, just four days after leaving London for New York. I came to attend graduate school, to get an MA in education and I had every intention of living my fantasy of the New York life. I'd come to the waterfront

150

that day with my cousin Bea and her eight-year-old daughter, Daria. I was staying in Bea's apartment, temporarily, but although we were first cousins, we hardly knew one another; Bea grew up in Jamaica and we had only met when my family went back for holidays. In an effort to break down the distance created by growing up so far apart, she was taking me out to see Brooklyn, to see the firework display, to see Manhattan from the Promenade, to introduce me to New York. Daria bounced and chattered every step of the short walk from the subway. She was thrilled by the crowd gathering to watch the display; the crowd that was already dense and thickening rapidly, layers of bodies packing the pathway. Daria jumped up and down, trying to see above rows of heads. She wanted to see the river and the pier on the other side. She jumped again and again, her beaded braids swinging, tireless as a jack-in the box despite her mother's restraining hand on her shoulder, despite the exhausting heat of the late afternoon. She stumbled against the man standing beside her, grazing his ankle with her sneaker. Bea is all polite apology, but the man shakes his shaven head and reaches tattooed arms to steady the child, with a half-smile and an *Easy there, young lady.*

By sunset, people were pressing against each other in hot, airless layers, so close that even Daria's restless energy was constrained. Bea made a game out of putting stories to the faces near us, faces that stood out because they were strangely beautiful, or strangely at odds with those around them: the bald-headed man with the tattooed arms, the Asian woman whose hand he cherished in his; the family group in front of us, a study of racial mixing, the grandparents white haired and white faced, the father dreadlocked coffee, the mother, the milkiest blonde, and their two denim-clad boys, golden *café au lait*.

The mix of the people pressing around us, the chatty, expectant mood, reminded me of the last time I was part of so large a crowd, many years before, in London, at Notting Hill carnival. That day, ranks of revellers, black, brown, white, blended, undulating, wavelike, one huge serpentine mass moving to carnival music, celebrating the joyous spirit of freedom under a greying English sky. In Brooklyn, we stood packed together, immobile witnesses to a magnificent show – noise, fire and colours that exploded gloriously across the sky. I felt constrained, confined to a space defined by people I did not know and who did not know me. I wondered if this was how I would feel living here, whether the life I dreamed of creating in this city famed for its pleasures and its freedoms would prove to be beyond my reach. Had I been seduced by a dream? A fantasy of a life sweetened with afternoons passed in cafés, long evenings drinking cocktails in jazz-clubs and nights at the movies? Would the fabled romance and delights of New York prove illusory, as evanescent as the fireworks that splashed the twilight sky and washed the dark river in light?

After the firework display we took the subway to Harlem, to the house of Bea's friend Diva, who was hosting a barbecue in the yard of her townhouse. We walked from the subway along Broadway, past groups of people gathered around domino tables, past groups of youths clustering on street corners, past restaurants bursting with families dressed in holiday clothes, shops bursting with cheap clothing, household goods and luggage, salsa music blasting out of each one. *We're in Spanish Harlem*, said Bea, explaining the obvious.

Diva's house was just off Broadway, on a well-kept block that sloped down towards Riverside Drive. Bea rang the bell and the door opened to another new world

– new to me, at least. As we made our way though the parlour toward the back-yard I glanced around me, admiring the raw silk curtains draped around the deep bay window, the tan leather sofa, the dark gloss on the hardwood floors. I was already impressed by the owner's taste.

Diva. Few women in the world lived up to such a name but Bea's friend was one of the few. Think tall, full-bodied, cocoa skin, and bronzed dreadlocks. Think black eyes alight with fun and a rich, full voice that sang even when she talked. I heard the voice first, raised above the chatter of people in the yard and the jazz that filled in the space between voices; it was a voice that evoked dim lighting, smoky rooms, and low, amorous conversations. Then I spotted her forking pieces of chicken onto a grill, wearing a long sleeveless dress of the lightest linen with a green *adinkara* motif printed around the hem. She hugged Bea, kissed Daria. When Bea introduced us, she smiled and looked me over. *Welcome to Harlem,* she said huskily. *Happy 4th of July.*

Bea and Daria disappeared into the house, leaving me to survey a well-dressed, well-groomed gathering: men in light-coloured shorts, dashikis, or bright, clean polo shirts; women in bold prints, long skirts, or light, floaty dresses, their bodies and hair scented with fragrant oils. And more dreadlocks than I had ever seen in one small space. It was the kind of company I had imagined in those new-place fantasies that filled the days before I left London for New York – the kind of company that I still dream of keeping. The smoky aroma of barbecued chicken mingled with a heady blend of wine and Blue Nile oil; the crescendo of laughing voices was underscored by the music and the steady drone of traffic from the street. Confidence seemed to shine from every face;

it was the stuff of glamour. I felt drawn, ached to belong, ready to be seduced.

The man is watching my face, a faint, expectant gleam in his eyes. I do not feel to explain; I am not in the mood for openness or confession. I turn his question back on him.

What about you; what brought you to New York?

His eyes close, he leans back against the bench. He breathes a deep sigh and his cheeks sink inwards; I can tell he is about to tell a story. I can tell he expects my sympathy. I wonder if he is an actor by profession.

I came here to be with my lover, he begins, and, again, I marvel at the openness of Americans. We came from LA. She got a job here as senior editor in a large publishing firm. We planned to start a new life, you could say, to get married eventually. I'm a writer – he looks at me with a slight, modest smile – we were in the same business, you could say. She was the love of my life. But we broke up after six months here.

He says all this simply, without embarrassment. Then he cradles the paper coffee cup in his hands and gazes deeply into the brown-black brew as though seeing the reflection of his lost love.

How did you know, I can't help asking. I can't help wondering what the signs of such a large love might be; how someone still quite young could know with such certainty that there would be no other equally important love at any time in the future.

He stares back at me, startled at my ignorance.

I would have done anything for her, gone anywhere to be with her, he says. Don't you know how it feels, to love someone like that?

Actually, no, I say, defiant, fighting a sudden, sweeping feeling of loss

There is a self-satisfied smile on his face and he speaks carefully, like a teacher with a particularly uncomprehending student.

She used to date my younger brother – he was totally wrong for her, nowhere near as smart as she is. She dumped him to be with me. And I left my wife to be with her.

I don't like the sound of this woman; I know people who behaved like that, using people then throwing them away. And though I don't really care about this man either, I feel obliged to ask, So, what went wrong?

He is all too eager to tell.

They had been living together for going on eight months, all that time frantically busy; she, settling in to the new job; he trying find part-time work, both of them adjusting to Manhattan. I understand that part well. The city demands that you adjust to its restless rhythms, to the hard edges of its people, to the claustrophobic atmosphere of its towering buildings. Then while they were both struggling to adjust, to the city, to each other – she started an affair with someone else.

I should have foreseen it, he says. She changed, so fast – but I thought it was only temporary, a reaction to all the stress. Even when she started snipping at me and picking fights, I put it all down to stress. She had always been kinda bitchy. Her tongue was knife-sharp, she could hurt your feelings in a second. If I just looked at her wrong when she was in a bad mood, she would curse me out – and she could curse like a sailor! (She could drink like one too, he adds, under his breath.) It would hurt like hell, I tell you but then she would, uh, kiss me and apologize and soothe the hurt with her voice, with just the right words.

He pauses for the space of a few breaths, eyes turned

towards the river with the vacant look of someone gazing into the past. I try to picture this woman who could keep a man's love by cursing him, by abusing him. I thought only women put up with pain of the kind this man is talking about. I thought only women were masochists. I'm thinking that she must have been special in some way, in looks maybe. Most likely, she was spectacular in bed.

I should've known she was treacherous, he said, shifting his gaze to my face. After all, she dumped my brother to be with me. It's just that I'd never met a woman so alive, so full of surprises. I never knew whether she would come home loving me or hating me. (I think there was violence somewhere in her background, though she would never admit it.)

I guess you're wondering how I could've loved a woman like that? he says, and I nod. He smiles and the lines around his eyes deepen, softening his face. She had the most beautiful hair. Brown and curly with reddish lights. And there was something magic about her voice that I loved; it could soothe away hurt and fatigue and pain. It was like the sound of a flute in your ears; it made you feel like you were sipping warm honey; it was all warm and mellow. It made you feel loved. That voice touched my heart like nothing else in my life has ever done.

The man pauses, watches my face, expecting a reaction.

Was she a Gemini? I ask.

No idea, he says, bemused.

I can't help but stare at this man, and marvel at his story, so strange it sounds like a romance novel, a movie, a soap opera. It made me wonder again about how people make a life. In America there are stories to follow, so many of them; the challenge is in choosing. As I begin to wonder what untold stories there might be out there in the world, waiting to guide and teach me, my belly rumbles, demanding breakfast.

I can tell you think I'm a romantic fool, he continues. Well, if it sounds that way, it's because it was all over long ago, and I've let go of the bad memories. But let me tell you how it ended.

I nod anticipating more drama. He tells good story; despite my hunger, I am interested.

On our last morning together we both got up early, around 7.00; I had an early meeting with an editor, she was going to the office. I remember waking with a heaviness in my head and a vague anxiety which I thought was all about the meeting. She was never good in the mornings and she started bitching at me about leaving the bathmat wet. Can you believe it? We got into a fight over the bathmat! And it really was a fight. I told her she was being unreasonable; she started on about how I always left the bathroom in a mess. And when I pointed out that she usually showered ahead of me, she just yelled, *Get out of my sight, you stupid fucker!* And then she punched me in the chest, and made to hit me again, but I blocked her arm and next thing, we were wrestling on the floor, making enough noise to wake the entire building. Can you picture it? Two intelligent, middleclass people rolling around the floor, kicking and pounding each other, like we were ignorant, and poor, and didn't know better. Cursing too, horribly, unforgivably. In the middle of it all I heard thudding on the floor – the people downstairs, banging with a broomstick. That brought us to our senses. We got up from the floor. I finished dressing and left the apartment. She didn't come home that night. The following weekend she came and packed up her things; that's when she told me she'd been seeing some-one else.

He speaks with such ease I suspect that I've heard a story that has been polished, edited, perfected by frequent telling. I wonder about the untold elements; the deserted first wife; the betrayed younger brother. I wonder about their stories.

When did this happen?

A month after the attack.

And we both look across the river, gazing into the space from which, just nine months earlier, the concrete towers of the World Trade Center had reached to the sky. A month after the attack. I recall it was an angry time. Couples separated, friendships crashed. Bea and I fought. All around me people fighting, like the man beside me on the bench and his lost lover. Bea had sent Daria back home, to our island, to stay with her sister for the Christmas holidays, to get her out of the edgy atmosphere of adult entropy. As I think of that time, I recall the previous night's dream and my race against the fire. My heart sinks, in a sad, leaden way I cannot account for.

I thought I'd never get over it, the man says quietly. The break-up, I mean.

And have you? I ask.

His lips twist into a smile. This city offers plenty of distractions.

I think he means movies, museums, and music, but then he says: There are a quarter million single, straight people in this city, most of them women… that's a lot of distraction.

How many of them are black? I ask.

He looks surprised.

I don't know, he says. I've never thought… probably the representative twelve percent. There's got to be plenty of choice for everyone. I mean to say, it's the world's largest dating market.

I take a while to absorb this information. The world's largest dating market. A quarter of a million straight single people. A heaving, teaming ocean of opportunity, you would think. So much opportunity, I have to wonder at the loneliness I see in the faces of people in the subway, on the street, in the elevator of the building where I live. Even this man, sitting beside me boasting of his distractions, is here, early on a Saturday morning, sitting on a bench on the Promenade, and not in a warm bed, wrapped in the arms of a lover. In this ocean of opportunity he is alone, I am alone.

The rhythmic squeak of stroller wheels interrupts the silence that has fallen. A child's urgent chatter floats in the air, pitched high above the sharp adult commands.

Heather, don't run, you'll fall!

Heather, come back here!

Male and female voices alternate. I turn to look and there she is, curls the colour of marigolds, hazel eyes shining as she skips towards me.

Hi! What's your name? Mine's Heather.

She claps her hand over her mouth and giggles, as though her name is a joke only she understands. She ignores the man beside me who is grinning, anticipating a greeting that she doesn't offer.

Well, hello! I reach over to ruffle the marigold curls, but before my hand makes contact, the stroller skids to a halt and the father scoops his daughter out of reach.

No Daddy, no!

I pull back my hand, stung, as though the father had lashed it with a whip. The child kicks and struggles and he puts her down, but he grips her wrist, pulling her along beside him. He is stocky and wears a weatherproof coat, and well-polished shoes. The woman, Heather's mother, I assume, is taller than he is. She glares at me so hard, I blush. The family walks past, the man dragging the child who keeps turning her head to look back at me.

My stomach growls and I pull my jacket tight around me. The sharp movement of my elbow jerks the half-empty cup of coffee from the man's hand onto the ground, splashing his sneakers.

I'm so sorry!

About the coffee? He stands, folding his paper, and retrieves the fallen cup. Don't worry, it was almost done, and it was cold, anyway. I'm going to get another one. Would you like…? His gaze fixes on my face.

The promise of a cup of coffee makes my stomach growl again. I look across the river at the grey sky. I notice how ominous and cold it appears now that the sun has taken its light behind a cloud. I feel the need for a little warmth, even if it comes in a cup, in the company of a stranger.

Ifeona Fulani holds a PhD in Comparative Literature from New York University and an MFA in Creative Writing, also from NYU. Her research interests include postcolonial literatures and cultures, feminisms and feminist literary theory. She is currently working on a manuscript titled *Black Women Reconfiguring the Black Atlantic*.

She was awarded a McCracken Fellowship by New York University's Department of Comparative Literature, 1999-2004; A Burke-Marshall Fellowship, New York University, Creative Writing Program, 1997-8; and a New York Times Foundation Creative Writing Fellowship, 1996-8. She teaches in the Liberal Studies Program at New York University.

She is the author of a novel, *Seasons of Dust* (1997) and editor of a volume of essays titled *Archipelagos of sound: Transnational Caribbeanities, Women and Music* (2012) which is due out in October. Her scholarly articles include, "The Caribbean Woman Writer and the Politics of Style", *Small Axe* 13, 2004; "Representing the Body of the New Nation in *The harder They Come* and *Rockers*", *Anthurium*, 2005; and "Gender, Conflict and Community in Gayle Jones' *Corregidora* and Jamaica Kincaid's *Lucy*", *Frontiers* 2011.

ACKNOWLEDGEMENTS

My first thanks go to Paule Marshall for her inspiration, guidance and support, without which these stories might not have been written. I am also grateful to the fellow writers with whom early versions of many of these stories were first shared – thanks especially to Ana Menendez, Kristen Martin, Angie Cruz, Natalie Darnforth, James Polchin and Chris Packard for their feedback and encouragement. Warmest thanks to Edwidge Danticat, Chuck Wachtel and Raymond Kennedy for their generosity in sharing their insight and experience.

Two of the stories in this book first appeared in the following publications:

"Precious and Her Hair" in *Black Renaissance/Renaissance Noire* (July 1999).
"Elephant Dreams" in *Small Axe* (March 2003).

OTHER NEW FICTION YOU MIGHT LIKE

Curdella Forbes
Ghosts
ISBN: 9781845232009; pp. 182; pub. 2012; price: £8.99

The circumstances of their brother's violent death inflicts such a wound on his family that its four oldest sisters feel compelled to come together to write, tell or imagine what led up to it, to unravel conflicting versions for the benefit of the younger generation of the huge Pointy-Morris clan.

From the richly distinctive voices of the writer Micheline (Mitch), who could never tell a straight truth, the self-contained and sceptical Beatrice (B), the visionary and prophetic Evangeline (Vangie), and the severely practical Cynthia (Peaches), the novel builds a haunting sequence of narratives around the obsessive love of their brother, Pete, for his dazzling cousin, Tramadol, and its tragic aftermath.

Set on the Caribbean island of Jacaranda at different points in a disturbing future, *Ghosts* weaves a counterpoint between the family wound and a world caught between amazing technological progress and the wounds global warming inflicts on an agitated planet.

In a lyrical flow between English and Jamaican Creole, *Ghosts* catches the ear and gently invades the heart. Love enriches and heals, but its thwarting is revealed as the most painful of emotions. Yet if deep sadness is at the core of the novel, there are also moments of exuberant humour

Diana McCaulay
Huracan
ISBN: 9781845231965; pp. 276; pub. 2012; price: £10.99

In the wake of her mother's death, Leigh McCaulay returns to Jamaica after fifteen years away in New York to find her estranged father and discover whether she has a place she can call home. Not least she must re-engage with the complexities of being white in a black country, of being called to account for the oppressive history of white slave owners and black slaves.

Interwoven with Leigh's return are the stories of two earlier arrivals, both from Scotland – of the future abolitionist Zachary Macaulay, who comes as a precocious youth of sixteen to work as a book-keeper on a sugar estate in 1786, and of John Macaulay who comes in 1886, a naive and sometimes self-deluding Baptist missionary, determined to bring light to the heathen.

"A sharp-eyed, salty-sweet mix of family history and historical fiction from Jamaica: Diana McCaulay has captured the bright tropic warmth, the violence and beauty of her birthplace like a born storyteller. Written in a vigorous, patois-inflected prose, *Huracan* scissors intriguingly backwards and forwards in time from the 1980s to the slave-driving 18th century. Over it all, hovers the figure of the Scottish abolitionist Zachary Macaulay, who came to the cane-cutting colony as a young man. Along the way, unforgettably, themes of homecoming, rootlessness and belonging are explored. All life is written in these haunting pages."
– Ian Thomson, author of *The Dead Yard: Tales of Modern Jamaica*

All books available online at www.peepaltreepress.com